Happy Birthday, Roger!

Love, Janet

No Place Like Home

A FANTASTICAL JOURNEY TO THE KINGDOM OF HEAVEN

Story by Jessie Beebe

Written and Illustrated by Janet Adele Bloss

LifeRich
PUBLISHING

Copyright © 2020 Janet Adele Bloss and Jessie Beebe.

All rights reserved. No part of this book may be used or reproduced by any means, graphic, electronic, or mechanical, including photocopying, recording, taping or by any information storage retrieval system without the written permission of the author except in the case of brief quotations embodied in critical articles and reviews.

Edited by: Jennifer Strickland

Co-illustrator: Wanda Geske

LifeRich Publishing is a registered trademark of The Reader's Digest Association, Inc.

LifeRich Publishing books may be ordered through booksellers or by contacting:

LifeRich Publishing
1663 Liberty Drive
Bloomington, IN 47403
www.liferichpublishing.com
1 (888) 238-8637

Because of the dynamic nature of the Internet, any web addresses or links contained in this book may have changed since publication and may no longer be valid. The views expressed in this work are solely those of the author and do not necessarily reflect the views of the publisher, and the publisher hereby disclaims any responsibility for them.

Any people depicted in stock imagery provided by Getty Images are models, and such images are being used for illustrative purposes only. Certain stock imagery © Getty Images.

This is a work of fiction. All of the characters, names, incidents, organizations, and dialogue in this novel are either the products of the author's imagination or are used fictitiously.

Scripture quotations marked (NIV) are taken from the Holy Bible, New International Version®, NIV®. Copyright © 1973, 1978, 1984, 2011 by Biblica, Inc.™ Used by permission of Zondervan. All rights reserved worldwide. www.zondervan.comThe "NIV" and "New International Version" are trademarks registered in the United States Patent and Trademark Office by Biblica, Inc.™

Scripture quotations marked (NLT) are taken from the Holy Bible, New Living Translation, copyright ©1996, 2004, 2015 by Tyndale House Foundation. Used by permission of Tyndale House Publishers, a Division of Tyndale House Ministries, Carol Stream, Illinois 60188. All rights reserved.

ISBN: 978-1-4897-2663-6 (sc)
ISBN: 978-1-4897-2662-9 (hc)
ISBN: 978-1-4897-2664-3 (e)

Library of Congress Control Number: 2020903155

Print information available on the last page.

LifeRich Publishing rev. date: 02/19/2020

This Book Belongs To

_____

DEDICATION

This book is dedicated to my mother and father,
Louise and Don Bloss, with love and gratitude.

Janet Adele Bloss

I dedicate this book to all the kids of Stand Ministries. Your creativity inspires me to allow God's purpose to flow onto these pages.

Jessie Beebe

"The wizard [of Oz] says look inside yourself and find self. God says look inside yourself and find [the Holy Spirit]. The first will get you to Kansas. The latter will get you to heaven. Take your pick."

— Max Lucado

CONTENTS

Chapter 1	Worst Day Ever	1
Chapter 2	Jesus, Where Are You?	7
Chapter 3	Princess Holly Sprite and the Munchkins	10
Chapter 4	Evileen, Chaos, and Fear	18
Chapter 5	The Tin Man	24
Chapter 6	Rainbows and Righteousness	32
Chapter 7	The Book of Wonderful Words	37
Chapter 8	Memories of Yesterday	40
Chapter 9	Darkness, Doubts, and Division	43
Chapter 10	The Scarecrow	54
Chapter 11	The Lion	61
Chapter 12	Friends to the Rescue	72
Chapter 13	Where Are We?	76
Chapter 14	Truth and Lies	82
Chapter 15	Home and the Kingdom	90

Afterword 95
Reader's Guide 97
About the Authors 103

CHAPTER 1

Worst Day Ever

DOROTHY raced into the house, through the hall, and back to her bedroom, where she flung open the door. A bright-green parakeet with blue cheeks jumped on a perch in her cage. The parakeet's eyes dilated as she squawked, "What up?"

"What up?" mimicked Dorothy. "Oh, Tutu, you won't believe it. *I* don't believe it." She put on her most forlorn face and spoke into the air. "Oh, how bitter is the wound from a trusted friend. How deep the pain from a lifelong BFF."

"Sweet sweet," said Tutu.

Dorothy looked back at her feathered friend. "Sweet? No. Not sweet at all. In fact, it was the opposite of—"

Ding!

Dorothy checked her cell phone. "You've got to be kidding me," she said. "It's a text from my ex-best friend, who is now my archnemesis." Her fingers darted across the keys, texting a reply in all caps: "NO, KIMMY, YOU CANNOT COME OVER! WE ARE NOT FRIENDS ANYMORE!"

She pushed send and then turned back to find Tutu pecking the feathers beneath her wing.

"Oh, Tutu, I have been betrayed."

"Sweet sweet."

"No, Tutu. It totally stinks. I was walking out of science today, and guess what I saw. Kimmy and Danny. Yes, *my* Danny, and my best friend, kissing next to the lockers. Kissing!"

"Squawk."

"Exactly."

No Place Like Home

Tutu whistled her signature eight-note melody, "Do-ray-me-fah-so-la-ti-do."

Dorothy opened the cage door, and Tutu stepped out onto her finger. "Six months we've been dating. Six months. And Kimmy didn't even like him when we first started dating. She said I could find someone better. Her exact words: 'someone better.'"

Tutu hopped from Dorothy's finger to the floor, where she scuttled toward a small, plastic ball that contained a jingle bell. Tutu pushed at the ball with her beak, delighted at the sound it made.

Dorothy threw herself onto her bed and stared up at the ceiling. "This is the worst day of my life," she moaned. "The worst day in the history of my entire existence."

The cheerful sound of a jingling bell broke through her thoughts. Dorothy looked at the bright-green and blue colors of her beloved parakeet and smiled, until she recognized a familiar squint of the eyes. "Please, Tutu," she said, "don't poop on the floor. I really can't take any more rejection today."

"Squawk."

The bird stood on one leg and then the other. The critical moment passed without incident. Tutu scuttled back across the floor to look up at Dorothy lying on her bed.

"At least we get to go to Dad's house. It's his weekend to have us. I've missed him so much. Better start packing."

Dorothy rolled off the bed, picked up Tutu, and placed her on her own shoulder, with a small protective towel beneath.

Dorothy pulled a suitcase out from under her bed.

"What up?" asked Tutu.

"Dad's house for the weekend," answered Dorothy. "A nice little getaway, and boy, do I need it."

"Dorothy, is that you?" her mother called from the kitchen.

"*Mommm!* You know I don't like to be called that." She hurried to the kitchen, feeling Tutu's claws grip tight on her shoulder.

"Sorry, baby," said her mom. "I mean, Dot. I mean D. Hey, don't worry about packing to go to your dad's. It's been canceled. He had to

Worst Day Ever

go out of town for work. It just came up. Looks like it's me, you, and Chad this weekend."

Dorothy rolled her eyes as far back into her head as humanly possible.

"Ugh. For real? How could this day get any worse? I can't escape. I don't have anyone to go out with this weekend."

"What about Kimmy? What about Danny?" asked her mother.

"I don't want to talk about it," Dorothy insisted. "It looks like I'm stuck with Chad and his Neanderthal buddies. Seriously, Mom, they practically drag their knuckles on the ground."

"Oh, Doro ... Dot ... D, it's not that bad."

"Have you smelled them lately?"

As if on cue, the kitchen door opened as Chad, Ross, and Jay tumbled into the room. They brought with them a cloud of dust and the smell of outdoors, denim, and football jerseys badly in need of washing. Jay, all hulking two hundred pounds of him, jumped in surprise when he saw the kitchen wasn't empty. He pushed his shaggy hair out of his eyes and said, "Hi, Mrs. K. Hey, Dot. You scared me. I didn't know anyone was here."

"Hello, boys," said Dorothy's mom. "I'm just here for a minute. I've got to get back to work. How was school?"

"I don't know," Chad said with a grin. "I didn't pay attention."

His mother shook her head and then turned to Ross, who lifted a heavy backpack from his shoulders and placed it on the floor. "Don't listen to him, Mrs. K.," Ross said. "School was great. I'm reading all of these books."

Dorothy wanted to wipe the self-satisfied look off of Ross's face, but she knew it was best to ignore him, or he would talk endlessly about all the books he was reading. This was what he did, and she found it best to not respond.

"Hey, sis. Hey, Toots," said Chad.

"Her name is Tutu. Show some respect."

"What up?" said Tutu. "Sweet sweet. Toodle-oo."

"Respect a bird? Uh, I don't think so. I mean, seriously, don't get so angry, D."

"What up?" mimicked Ross.

"Sweet," said Jay.

The boys laughed so hard that Dorothy wondered hopefully if the excessive hilarity might result in a medical emergency. She felt even worse when she saw her mother stifling a smile.

"It's just a bird," said Chad.

"Just a bird?" Dorothy said. "I don't think so, my illiterate brother. Tutu is a parakeet. Also known in the rest of the world as a budgerigar, or budgie for short. The scientific name is *Melopsittacus undulatus.*"

"Uh, yeah, brainiac. It's a bird," Chad joked as his friends began a new round of laughter.

It was Dorothy whose feathers were ruffled as she answered, "Well, she's a whole lot smarter than you and your little squad of geniuses."

"We don't have time for this. We gotta raid the fridge for some protein." Chad threw open the refrigerator door as Dorothy left the kitchen at what she hoped was a dignified pace.

"Toodle-oo," Tutu called from Dorothy's shoulder.

The boys began howling with laughter again, and it was one of the few times that Dorothy wished that her budgie had remained silent.

Back in her room, Dorothy closed the door and began a heart-to-heart with her bright-green *Melopsittacus undulatus.*

"What am I gonna do, Tutu? I've lost my best friend and my boyfriend in one single day."

4

Worst Day Ever

Ding!

A quick look at her phone showed another text from Kimmy.

"*What?* No way. Kimmy is here, actually here at my house. Outside. I do not want to talk to her."

Dorothy peeped through her bedroom window, careful not to disturb the curtain. "She's here. Kimmy's on our front porch."

The ding from the phone was followed by a volley of chimes from the doorbell.

Dorothy heard her mother open the front door and say, "Hi, Kimmy. Come in. Dot's in her room. Go on back. She'll be glad to see you. What a nice surprise."

Dorothy heard footsteps and then the door swung cautiously open. There stood Kimmy in the pink leggings that she always wore, a sheepish look on her face.

Dorothy's distraught ex-best friend entered the room and began a breathless apology. "I am *sooooo* sorry, D. It just happened. You know how Danny and I have algebra together. Well, we started studying every day after school, and well, we just spent so much time together, and it just happened. D, don't hate me. *Please?*"

"Are you serious?" exclaimed Dorothy. Tutu gave her a concerned peck on the ear. "You went behind my back. You never told me you two were hanging out. And *kissing? Kissing?*"

"It just happened that one time," insisted Kimmy.

"Right. Sure. And I just happened to be there to see it. Seriously, am I supposed to believe that?"

"It's true," insisted Kimmy.

"One time is one time too many. How can I ever trust you again?" asked Dorothy. "Here you are, acting like we should still be BFFs, and the whole time you were being so evil."

"Evil? That's a little much, don't you think?"

"No, I don't. Evil is exactly what you are. I can't trust you. I don't want you here anymore. *Leave,*" she insisted, arms folded across her chest.

"But—"

"I said leave. I can't believe you have the nerve to think—"

At that moment, Tutu made a hop from Dorothy's shoulder to Kimmy's.

Dorothy gasped, and her mouth stayed open for a moment longer than was necessary.

Kimmy ran a gentle finger down Tutu's back. "Hi, pretty girl," she said.

"Et tu, Tutu?" asked Dorothy, who was studying *The Life and Death of Julius Caesar* in school. "Et tu?" She reached out, lifted the bird from Kimmy's shoulder, and then returned her to the perch in her cage. To Kimmy she said, "What you did to me is unforgivable. Get out." She opened her bedroom door, gave Kimmy a push, then slammed the door, leaning heavily against it.

She listened intently, waiting to feel if there might be any pushback. Instead, she heard footsteps run down the hall, and then the front door opened and slammed shut.

Plopping down onto her bed of sorrow, Dorothy whispered into her pillow, "Why is all of this happening to me? Okay, Jesus, we gotta talk. What is going on? I *know* there is more to life than all this junk. If I believe in you, I'm supposed to be happier, right? I'm not supposed to be so angry and disappointed. We learned Wednesday at youth to pursue the kingdom. What even *is* the kingdom? The pastor said it's something about peace and joy. I could really use some peace and joy right now, Lord. Ugh. Tutu, how could this day get any worse?"

Her question was answered immediately by the shrill of a tornado siren.

CHAPTER 2

Jesus, Where Are You?

DOROTHY jumped up from her bed, tore open the door, and ran into the living room, arriving at the same moment as Chad, Ross, and Jay. The emergency siren screamed from their cell phones.

"Do you hear that?" asked Chad. "There's a tornado right in our area."

"I read that tornadoes can reach wind speeds of up to 300 miles per hour," Ross said. "I hope that this isn't a multiple-vortex tornado. I've read those are the worst."

Jay shook his shaggy head. "I didn't need to know that, bro," he said.

"Where's Mom?" asked Dorothy.

"She already left for work," said Chad. "I hope she's not caught on the road in this storm. Maybe I should call her. Or maybe we should take cover first. Or we could open the windows. Or I could call Mom. Or I could call Dad. Or …"

"Focus, Chad. Focus," Dorothy said. "Let's think this through."

Jay's voice rose to a pitch remarkably close to that of a little girl as he pushed his long hair out of his eyes. "We have to find somewhere for shelter."

Dorothy stared at Jay, surprised that the biggest, most muscular of the three boys sounded the most frightened.

"Where are your emergency tornado drill instructions?" asked Ross.

"Our what?" asked Dorothy. "Chill, Ross, y'all, we get tornado warnings every five minutes during this season, and they never actually happen."

"Hey, Einstein, it's a sighting, not a warning," said Chad.

No Place Like Home

"Uh-oh," said Ross. "Dr. Wiseman's research on tornadoes show that some paths of destruction can be up to one mile wide and fifty miles long. Dr. Wiseman also reported that the worst tornado in history was in 1989 in Bangladesh. Over thirteen hundred people were killed."

"Hey," Jay said, nervously. "Give Dr. Wiseman a call and ask him what we're supposed to do, okay?"

"Just trying to help," said Ross. "Being informed is the best defense against disaster. It's always good to hear what the experts have to say."

"We're not writing a paper, Ross," said D. "We're in a real situation here. We need to take action."

Chad looked at the ominous black clouds forming outside.

"Get away from the window," Jay ordered.

Chad turned to his sister and said, "Hey, Dot, you better pray to that Jesus you're always talking about. It's starting to look pretty serious out there."

To herself, Dorothy thought, *Pray to Jesus? I'm not sure where Jesus has been today. Can I talk to him when he doesn't seem to be nearby? Maybe he's just not listening. Or maybe I'm not choosing the right words to talk to him. Or ... or ... I don't know.*

Ross, reading from his cell phone said, "According to the weather station, our safest place is under the stairs."

Jay, struggling to get his voice under control, shouted, "Under the stairs. Under the stairs. Everybody get into the coat closet."

"Wait. I've got to get Tutu." Dorothy ran back to her room, grabbed the cage, and hurried back to the living room. The budgie squawked with each running step, swinging wildly on her little trapeze.

Dorothy saw that her brother was standing by the front door. "Get under the stairs," she yelled.

"No way," shouted Chad. "First, I'm gonna get a video. Look! It's coming. Check this out." He threw open the front door and held up his camera phone.

It was as if a gigantic arm of wind reached into the house. Its angry fingers spread into every corner, throwing leaves and papers. To Dorothy's horror, it was at that exact moment that the cage door popped open, and Tutu tumbled out. The little parakeet was swallowed up

Jesus, Where Are You?

in a swirl of debris. Too frightened to make a noise, Dorothy's green-feathered pet was swept out of the front door, disappearing into low, moving clouds.

"Noooooo," screamed Dorothy. "No." She stepped outside into the blustering wind.

"Get back here. Are you crazy?" cried Chad. He grabbed Dorothy's arm, pulling her into the house. "She's gone, Dorothy. Tutu's gone. There's nothing we can do about it."

It took the shoulder strength of Chad and Ross to push the door shut and lock it.

"Come on," Jay yelled above the roar of the wind. He had already squeezed his bulky body into the space beneath the stairs, in the closet. "We're gonna die."

Chad pulled a stunned Dorothy into the closet and pushed her onto the floor. He crawled in after her, with Ross following.

The four sat squashed together, arms around their knees, beneath the stairs in the dark. Dorothy felt the soft flannel of Chad's shirt against her arm. They heard solid objects, driven by the wind, hitting the roof. Outside, the kitchen screen door slapped again and again, then ripped from its hinges.

"I'm sorry, Dot," said Chad." I'm so sorry about Tutu. I guess I wasn't thinking. I wasn't paying attention. I didn't mean to ..."

Dorothy pressed her hands over her ears, rested her elbows on her knees, and tried not to think about the little bird snatched away by the howling wind. She said nothing, just closed her eyes and wished over and over that she was any place but where she was.

CHAPTER 3

Princess Holly Sprite and the Munchkins

WHEN Dorothy opened her eyes, she was surprised to find that the dark of the closet had been replaced by a flowing mist of rainbow colors: red, orange, yellow, green, blue, indigo, and violet. Bright yet soft colors streamed around her.

"Chad? Ross? Jay?"

They were nowhere to be seen. Rather, she found herself sitting in an open clearing, dotted with flowers and surrounded by dense forest. From the trees came the sound of birdsong.

"Tutu?" she called, hopefully. She turned her head and was surprised to find herself staring up into the green eyes of a young woman who looked like a princess. A crown of green leaves and red berries sat atop her silver hair. Tiny silver bells tinkled with the movement of her graceful arm. From her shoulders to the ground fell robes of rainbow colors.

"What's going on?" Dorothy jumped to her feet, standing face-to-face with this royal vision of grace. Should she bow, curtsey, or run away? Broken sentences escaped her lips like popcorn popping. "What? ... Where? ... Who? ... Why? ... No way ... This is ... This isn't ... Who are ...?"

The divine being announced herself, saying, "My name is Princess Holly Sprite." A gentle smile lit up her serene face. "It is so nice to make your acquaintance, Miss Dorothy."

"My name isn't Dorothy."

"Isn't that the name your parents gave to you?"

Princess Holly Sprite and the Munchkins

"Well, yes, it is. But Dot is so much faster to say, and D is even faster and shorter to spell. And I guess I just like the name D better."

"Then D it is," said Princess Holly Sprite. Her rainbow robes rustled as a little man stepped out from behind her. He was a small person indeed, about the size of a fire hydrant.

"Yikers," Dorothy exclaimed and jumped back.

With a quick salute, the little man, a gnome, said, "Hello, D. Can we be friends?"

Dorothy stared at his long white beard, which reached his knees. "I'm not sure," she said. "Who are you?"

A second little man stepped forward, saying, "That's my brother Harry. My name is Pipken." Pipken's gray beard was so long that he had braided it and wrapped it around his waist. Pipken removed the pointed hat from his head and made a bow so grand that his nose touched the ground. "Greetings and salutations, Miss D," he said.

"What's going on?" asked Dorothy. It was all happening so fast. It felt a bit like when one somersaults down a long hill in the sunshine, just for the fun of it, then stands up, twirls, and tries to walk in a straight line, but instead falls laughing to the ground.

Only, Dorothy wasn't laughing.

"Greetings and salutations," Pipken repeated.

Harry explained, "Salutations. That means best wishes, kind regards, a respectful hello."

"Then why didn't he just say that?" asked Dorothy.

"My brother Pipken has a fine vocabulary, and he likes to use it," Harry said.

"A more elegant how-do-you-do seemed appropriate on this auspicious occasion," Pipken said, returning his hat to his head.

"All righty then," Dorothy said, doubtfully. She looked at Princess Holly Sprite. "Is this for real?" she asked. "Don't tell me that these are …"

"Munchkins!" A chorus of voices rang from the woodland, as dozens of small faces peered from behind the trees, and an army of little feet skipped across the grass. Laughing and tumbling, the little people approached Dorothy and the princess. Their sizes ranged from

No Place Like Home

short to shorter. The men wore pointed hats. The little women wore blue skirts, multicolored scarves tied around their heads, and wooden shoes.

As they skipped out from the shadows, they appeared to be surrounded by moving waves of rainbow air: red, orange, yellow, green, blue, indigo, and violet. The many-hued light had its source from Princess Holly Sprite, who smiled lovingly at the excited group.

"Seriously?" asked Dorothy. She turned to Princess Holly Sprite. "Pretty cute, but kind of cliché, don't you think? Munchkins? Just because my name is Dorothy?"

Pipken looked confused. "So your name really is Dorothy? I thought you said it wasn't. Do you want us to refer to you less formally, perhaps by your chosen moniker of D?"

Now it was Dorothy's turn to be confused. "Did I choose a moniker?"

"Yes," explained Harry. "It's another of my brother's vocabulary words."

Pipken explained, "A moniker is a descriptive or familiar name given, instead of or in addition to, the one belonging to an individual."

"You mean a nickname?" asked Dorothy.

"Precisely," said Pipken.

"Then why didn't you just say so?"

"I told you that my brother has a very fine vocabulary," Harry said. "He graduated from the Munchkin Academy of Extensive Knowledge."

Dorothy's thoughts whirled. Input overload. It was all a jumble of new words and new worlds. "Let me get this straight. You're Princess Holly Sprite, right?" asked Dorothy.

"Yes, my love."

"So ... you aren't the Good ..."

"Oh, yes, I am good all right. In fact, I am as good as they come. I'm here to be your friend, counselor, and helper on your journey."

"What journey?" asked Dorothy.

The munchkins giggled as the princess explained, "Well, beloved, you have just arrived in the Land of the Seekers, haven't you?"

"Land of the what?"

"Seekers," said Harry.

Princess Holly Sprite and the Munchkins

"Seekers are seeking something," said Pipken. "Looking for ... searching ... trying to find ... in quest of ..."

"I know what 'seeking' means," Dorothy said, perhaps a bit too snappishly. "Thank you very much. But how am I supposed to seek after something when I don't even know what I'm looking for?"

Princess Holly Sprite laid her hand gently on Dorothy's shoulder. "Oh, you *must* know what you are seeking."

Dorothy took a deep breath. "Sure. I'm seeking my bird Tutu. That's all. I think. But now that you mention it, I am seeking a new BFF and a new boyfriend."

A gentle breeze ruffled Princess Holly Sprite's robes. She looked thoughtful. "Hmmm ... I think it's time for our very first counseling session."

"With who?" asked Dorothy.

"Whom," corrected Pipken.

Dorothy shot him a stink eye.

"With me, Princess Holly Sprite. Counseling is just one of the things that I do."

Dorothy nodded her head. "Oh ... I get it. Your last name is Sprite. You're Holly Sprite. Hold up." She paused to think. "Counselor, helper, friend. I think I'm getting the metaphor here. Holly Sprite ... Holly ... *Holy Spirit?*"

Princess Holly winked and nodded. She walked across the grass and came to a stone bench inlaid with emeralds, sparkling green in the sunlight. As she sat down, her slender hand patted the empty space beside her, encouraging D to sit beside her.

The munchkins parted like the Red Sea as Dorothy passed through, joining the princess on the jeweled bench.

Princess Holly asked, "So, D, can you please explain to me what happened right before you arrived in the Land of the Seekers? What was going on in your life?"

Dorothy sighed, not wanting to think back to the dark hours before she found herself in this strange place. "Nothing much. Well ... unless you mean my whole world falling apart. Let me review. Do I have a best friend? No, not anymore. Do I have a boyfriend named Danny? No, I don't think so. Do I have a favorite pet named Tutu, who trusts me to take care of her and keep her safe?" A tear slid from Dorothy's eye, all the way down her cheek, dropping onto the toe of her green sneaker. "No. Tutu's gone. Because I didn't take care of her. My favorite pet and possibly only friend, pathetic as that is. She went bye-bye. Then there's my home. You know, a house with a roof? Not there anymore. That's why I'm here. Because a tornado blew everything to smithereens."

"Where's Smithereens?" asked Harry.

Pipken answered, "I believe that Smithereens is near Fort Worth, Texas, USA. The latitude is 32.768799, and the longitude is -97.309341."

"Possibly," Dorothy said, looking doubtful. She shook her head sadly. "I honestly don't know where anything is anymore." She searched the landscape around her: field, trees, Princess, munchkins. "I also don't know where my mother is, or where my brother Chad, Ross, and Jay are. Are they here somewhere? Are they with Tutu?"

Princess Holly looked deeply into Dorothy's eyes. The young girl saw the tiny reflection of herself in the royal eyes. She also saw kindness, gentleness, and strength.

"All in good time, beloved, all in good time. Hmmm. Let's see. Can you tell me what happened before the tornado? Did you perhaps say anything to the Big Boss in the sky? The Forever King?"

Dorothy shrugged her shoulders. "Big Boss in the Sky? Forever King?"

Princess Holly's laughter blended with the sound of silver bells as she answered, "You know. My boss. The Big Boss." She adjusted her holly-laden crown, flipping a long curl of silver hair from her shoulder.

"Oh," Dorothy said, "Okay. If you're the Holy Spirit, then your boss must be … God. Wow. Holy Spirit … God. Got it. Ummm, actually, yes, I did have a few words with Him."

"Whatever did you say?" The twinkle in Holly's eye told Dorothy that the princess already knew what Dorothy had said, but she wanted to hear it from her own lips.

"Well," Dorothy began, forming her hands into fists in her lap. "I think I mentioned what a junky day it's been. I mean, the worst. I told God about how I caught my best friend since preschool kissing …

Princess Holly Sprite and the Munchkins

kissing ... my boyfriend, who happens to be the first boyfriend I've ever had. And who happens to be someone that my former best friend once said I shouldn't date because I could do better. So if she thinks he's not good enough for me, why is she kissing him? And if he's my boyfriend, why is he kissing her? Also, how can my former ex-best friend show up at my house and expect me to act like nothing even happened? So, yeah, I talked to God about all of this stuff and told him I really needed some help and guidance. Did I get help and guidance? Nope. My house got wrecked in a tornado, and my sweet, trusting little parakeet, my only friend in the world, who weighs exactly 2.2 ounces, got sucked out of my house into a tornado. Thanks a lot, God. That's all I've got to say."

"That's all?" asked Princess Holly Sprite.

"I'm not going to cry," Dorothy said, wiping her eyes. "I'm not going to cry. I told God that there has to be more to this life. We learned at church about the Kingdom of God and how it's at hand. Well, it definitely doesn't seem like it's at *my* hand. I mean, what does that even mean? Isn't the Kingdom of God heaven? Where we go when we die? So how is the kingdom here right now too? It's in heaven, *and* it's here on earth? That just doesn't make any sense. How can the kingdom be in two places at the same time?"

Princess Holly took Dorothy's hands in her own. "Then that, my love, is why you are here in the Land of the Seekers. You are seeking the Kingdom of Heaven on earth, also known as the Kingdom of God. Look ahead."

Dorothy raised her eyes to the trees and then looked up above the forest. In the far, far distance, she saw a sky tinted with the color of gold. She heard birds singing, and she couldn't be sure, but she thought she heard a familiar eight-note melody.

"Tutu?"

As she stared and listened, the distant sky seemed to take on the color of hope. From the sound of birdsong overhead came notes of encouragement. Dorothy rose from the glittering emerald bench.

"Is that where I'm supposed to go?" she asked. "Into the forest?"

"Yes, beloved," Princess Holly answered amid the tingling of silver bells. "If you wish to discover the Kingdom of God, you must go there."

No Place Like Home

"I will," said Dorothy. "I really will. Maybe I can get some answers there."

"It's a journey," Princess Holly Sprite reminded her. "You, beloved, will have many choices to make as you travel. Will you pursue the kingdom, or will you give up, as many before you have done?"

Dorothy squared her shoulders. "Give up? You don't know me. Not *this* girl. I *never* give up. I've got this." Finger snap.

Princess Holly Sprite took Dorothy by the hand and began walking toward the dark forest. The munchkins followed, calling, "You can do it, D. We know you can."

"Be careful, D," said Harry.

"Be stalwart and persevere in your travails," added Pipken.

They arrived at the edge of the dark, dark forest where two paths began, both paved with yellow brick. One path was narrow, just wide enough for one little lamb at a time to walk upon it. The other path was wide enough for a whole herd of goats, plus an elephant or two.

With a sweep of her hand, Princess Holly indicated the two paths, saying, "Choose a path for your journey, beloved. This is the wide path that leads to destruction. This is the narrow path that leads to life. Which do you choose?"

Princess Holly Sprite and the Munchkins

"Duh," exclaimed Dorothy. "Seems like a no-brainer to me. Who would ever choose the path to destruction?"

"You'd be surprised," sighed the princess. "Look more closely." Dorothy peered down the path of destruction, which curved and faded into the trees. In the distance among the shadows, she saw something, which sparkled. Diamonds? Gold? Stars? The sight of possible treasure in the distance tickled her curiosity. It seemed to call to her with the promise of a jackpot, adventure, excitement. The urge to take a step onto that path was strong, but she reminded herself that every word from Princess Holly Sprite's mouth was pure truth. This heaven-sent truth would be her guide. She stepped toward the narrow path, feeling instant relief at having made her first choice.

Suddenly, there was a smell of sulfur. "Excuse me," said Harry. "I had tuna for lunch."

"It's not you, my brother," said Pipken. "It's the noxious odor that portends the imminent arrival of evil herself."

"Evileen! Evileen!" the munchkins cried in fear. They drew as close to Princess Holly Sprite as they could, like frightened sheep around a shepherd.

CHAPTER 4

Evileen, Chaos, and Fear

A cloud of brown, swirling smoke descended from the sky. From its depths stepped a creature in red leggings.

"Kimmy," exclaimed Dorothy. As the smoke cleared, a closer look revealed the black pointed hat, tattered black dress, and broom of a witch. The purple skin was a clue too, along with orange eyes and a grape-sized wart on the tip of her long nose. "For a minute, I thought you were …"

"Who, my dear? Who did you think I was?" A ghastly smile revealed pointed teeth.

"Uh … well … my ex-BFF," stammered Dorothy.

"Oh, how delightful." Evileen rubbed her claw-like fingers together. "What a wonderful idea. You and I as BFFs. It could happen. Couldn't it? What do you think, Fear?"

She spoke to the large crow on her shoulder, who answered, "B-b-best friends. Y-yes. That would b-be p-perfect."

Evileen spoke next to the crow on her other shoulder. "And you, my dear Chaos. Do you think D and I would make a lovely pair?"

Chaos croaked his answer: "Little D has come to thee. Join hands in camaraderie, together forever in darkness and pitch, a silly young lady and an old evil witch."

"I don't like the sound of that," said Dorothy. She looked confused and glanced at Princess Holly Sprite, who stood by quietly, unperturbed, a gentle smile on her face. Her fearless presence gave Dorothy the courage to ask, "What do you want?"

Evileen, Chaos, and Fear

"What do *I* want?" asked Evileen. "Why, I want nothing, my friend. I want to give you whatever *you* want. I want to give you my friendship, to guide you through the deep, dark, dangerous forest. Why? Because I see that you are about to take the wrong path."

Fear whispered, "D-d-deep ... d-d-dark ... d-d-dangerous."

Chaos screeched, "Wandering and lonely into the cold night, not even a candle to give you a light. Each little step can end in a cost. Helpless and hopeless and forever lost."

Evileen's lips stretched over her pointed teeth in a smile worthy of a Halloween pumpkin. "Oh, sweet little D. I've been waiting for you."

"Waiting for me?" asked Dorothy. "I seriously doubt that. You look more like you're waiting for someone to take you clothes shopping. That dress is so last century."

Chaos pecked at Evileen's cobweb hair; the crow pulled out a beetle and swallowed it.

"Gross," Dorothy exclaimed. She stood tall, placing her fists on either side of her waist. "I know what you're here for, Evileen, and it's not to be my friend. It's not to help me."

"Look down the wide path, my dear," urged the witch. "See how it sparkles?"

The wide winding path into the forest did indeed sparkle in the distance. It seemed to promise something wonderful. For a moment, Dorothy longed to discover what it might be. Then she gave herself a resolute shake and said, "I'm not falling for your tricks. You're here to take me down the wrong path. You're nothing more than a witch. A very wicked witch. I can't trust you."

"The broad path offers adventure," promised Evileen. She tried to widen her eyes into a look of innocence. "Trust me," she wheedled. "I'll walk beside you. I'm so lonely. You are too, right?"

"T-t-t-trust her," whispered Fear.

"How can I trust you if you have 'evil' in your name?" asked Dorothy.

"Oh, that," answered Evileen. "It is an unfortunate circumstance of my birth that I received that name. I plan to change it legally once my attorney gets out on probation."

"Sure. The name Evileen makes it pretty obvious who you are, don't you think?" asked Dorothy.

Princess Holly's silver hair fell like a curtain as she bent to whisper into Dorothy's ear, "Evil doesn't always choose to seem so obvious. Evileen can change her looks. Sometimes, she appears as things you desire or want. You must be careful, D; she changes forms. She will confuse and manipulate the truth."

Pipken said solemnly, "To manipulate. This means to exploit, maneuver, engineer, falsify, influence cleverly, unfairly, or unscrupulously. To distort."

"I know what manipulate means," Dorothy cried. "What are you guys? Munchkins or dictionaries?"

Princess Holly laid a calming hand on Dorothy's head. "As I was saying, Evileen will manipulate the truth. She can confuse you."

"Oh, my, my," Evileen protested. "Don't listen to that boring goody two-shoes. She wouldn't know fun if it knocked on her front door. Just choose my easy-peasy wide path, and I will get you a boyfriend. The boyfriend you always wanted: Danny."

Evileen, Chaos, and Fear

"Danny Martinez?" asked Dorothy, surprised. "You know Danny? My boyfriend?"

"Of course," said Evileen. "Danny and I are good friends."

"I don't believe you," said Dorothy. "Danny is a nice boy."

"Not too nice to kiss your best friend, was he?" asked Evileen.

A sorrow, temporarily stilled, pulsed back to life in Dorothy's heart. "Yeah," she said. "He did that. He's not really as nice as I thought he was."

"Don't let her confuse you," whispered Princess Holly. "This isn't about Danny. This is about who *you* are."

"I'll give you Danny," said Evileen. "I can get him back for you."

"I don't want him," said Dorothy.

"Oh, don't you?" asked Evileen. "Wouldn't you like to prove to Kimmy that Danny likes you best? That would put her in her place. *Or* you could get Danny back, then dump him. That would feel pretty good, wouldn't it? After what he did to you? Think about it, dearie."

"D-do what she says," croaked Fear. "She has p-p-power."

Chaos nodded.

Dorothy thought about how great it would feel for Kimmy to see Danny come crawling back. She imagined the power she could have over Danny, power to make him love her madly and then to break his heart, just like he had broken hers. She stepped toward the wide path.

"That's my good girl," said Evileen. "Everything will turn out all right if you just take my advice. I promise. You can get Danny back and stay with him, or get him back and kick him to the curb. That would feel good, wouldn't it? Revenge is so sweet."

Dorothy took another step toward the wide path but then turned to look at Princess Holly Sprite. The moment their eyes connected, Dorothy saw the truth and recognized the lies coming from Evileen and her wicked crows. She stopped herself abruptly. "Whoa," she gasped. "This is not good." Her eyes on Princess Holly, she said, "You were right. They sure make that wide path look good. I almost chose the wrong path without even realizing it."

"You were manipulated," cried Harry.

Pipken added, "Cleverly influenced, exploited, tricked, bamboozled."

No Place Like Home

"All right already. I get it." Dorothy placed her green-sneakered foot onto the narrow yellow path.

Princess Holly Sprite nodded, her silver hair and rainbow robes shining in the twilight, for the day was growing long. "Yes. Evileen and her crows can be quite convincing, my love. Sometimes, they look beautiful. Sometimes, they sound lovely. Remember, choosing the narrow path doesn't mean you won't receive any of those things that look pleasing to you. The narrow side puts love, joy, and peace in front of those things."

"Wait," Evileen cried, her composure cracking, one red legging sliding down to her ankle. "Who needs love, joy, and peace when you can have …"

"F-f-fame and f-fortune," said Fear.

Chaos rolled his black head on his neck and shrilled, "Have control over them, your friend and your boy. They'll be in your power. Revenge is a joy."

"You'll get your pride back," promised Evileen. "Both Danny and Kimmy will beg you to take them back. When you think about it, it's only fair."

Dorothy sighed and stepped back onto the grass, looking from one path to the other. "This isn't easy," she said.

"Sometimes, it's not," said Princess Holly Sprite. "So, beloved, which path will you take? It is completely your choice."

The munchkins, led by Pipken and Harry, began to shout in chorus, "Narrow path, narrow path, narrow path!"

"Yes, it is completely your choice," snarled Evileen, smiling her pointy-toothed smile. She stared meaningfully at Fear and then Chaos, and shrugged her shoulders. The crows, their black feathers gleaming in the setting sun, flew, one to Dorothy's left shoulder and the other to her right shoulder. Together, they began to whisper, "Ch-ch-choose the wide path. Do-it-do-it-do-it-do-it. T-take the dark path. Do-it-do-it-do-it."

Back and forth, back and forth, Dorothy turned her head, listening, listening. Suddenly, she pushed the crows off her shoulders, yelling,

Evileen, Chaos, and Fear

"No. I'm not listening to you. I choose life. I choose light. I choose the narrow path."

The air was filled with the screeching of two angry crows, the cries of one crazy witch, and the happy shouts of dozens of dancing munchkins. Through it all, Dorothy heard the still, quiet voice of Princess Holly Sprite, saying, "Well done, D. Well done."

Chaos, from the safety of Evileen's shoulder, said, "You're just a girl and a small one at that. You got lost in a closet. Do you know where you're at? You had a pet. She's lost too. She's flying and crying and looking for you."

Dorothy felt her heart sink at the thought of her lost and helpless Tutu.

"Don't listen," said Holly Sprite. "The crows are just trying to scare you. Remember that Evileen and her crows are liars. You can't believe anything they say. They often mix truth with lies."

Evileen's pointed teeth came together as she growled, "You'll regret this."

With Chaos and Fear on each of her shoulders, Evileen climbed onto her broom and rose into the sky amid a noxious, brown funnel cloud. The munchkins held their noses. Higher and higher she rose, until she was far above the treetops.

The sun fell behind the horizon, just as Dorothy heard Evileen's last shrieking words fading into the dusk, "You haven't seen the last of me, my girl. Just you wait. I'll be back."

CHAPTER 5

The Tin Man

IT'S not easy to sleep at night when all in one day, you have experienced the treachery of a best friend, unfaithfulness of a boyfriend, loss of a beloved pet, destruction of one's home, waking up in a parallel universe, hate speech from two crows, and a confrontation with an evil witch. This was true for Dorothy as she lay, exhausted before the narrow path, just outside the forest. Even though the witch and her crows had disappeared into the night sky, Dorothy still seemed to feel Fear and Chaos fluttering through her mind. She looked up into the gentle eyes of Princess Holly Sprite, who without saying a word let Dorothy know that she would never leave her.

The princess knelt in the grass beside the dark forest. She reached a hand up to Dorothy and pulled her gently down. Dorothy rested her head in the princess's rainbow lap. Fireflies twinkled in the field beyond. Stars filled the sky. Points of light flashed everywhere throughout the darkness, around and above.

She closed her eyes, and her mind drifted to dreams of a sweet little voice saying, "What up? Toodle-oo."

With the dawn, Dorothy awoke in anticipation of a new day and a continued adventure into the unknown. Into those happy thoughts, a ragged memory intruded, screaming, "You'll regret this. You haven't seen the last of me."

"Focus on what is beautiful," said Princess Holly. "Don't let fear and memories pull you back into pain."

Dorothy stood up, stretched, and brushed the grass from her jeans. "I'm still not completely understanding any of this," she confessed.

The Tin Man

Princess Holly shook her head, the sound of small bells filling the air. "Oh, you'll never understand all of it until you reach the forever kingdom. Wanting to understand all of it is where many get tripped up. Take our friend over there." She pointed into the forest to a man made of tin, sitting on a big book, surrounded by papers and magazines. In his hands, he held a book, turning a page with a pointed metal finger.

"You've got to be kidding me," exclaimed Dorothy. "This can't be happening. Don't tell me that's the Tin …?"

"Uh-huh. Tin Man," said Princess Holly.

"Tin is a silvery-white metal, the chemical element of atomic number 50," came a voice from above.

"Pipken?" Dorothy looked up to see Pipken and Harry resting comfortably in the tree branches just inside the woods. Quick as cats, they scrambled down to the ground.

"This adventure gets weirder and weirder," said Dorothy.

"Is that a bad thing?" asked Princess Holly.

"I'm not sure," said Dorothy. "If I'm in the story I think I am, shouldn't I be meeting a scarecrow just about now?"

"This is *your* story," said Holly Spirit. "No one else's. No one else has a story exactly like yours. No one ever has or ever will. Things will happen in their own way and time."

Dorothy bent to tighten the laces of her green sneakers. "Well, I've gotten this far. I guess I'll just go with it." She took a deep breath and stepped onto the narrow path with Princess Holly. Together, they walked beneath a canopy of branches.

"Good morning, Tin," called the princess.

The shiny metal man closed his book and looked up. "Princess Holly Sprite," he exclaimed, jumping to his feet in a clatter of metal on metal. The sound reminded Dorothy of carrying a bag of recycled cans.

"Tin, I'd like you to meet a young woman who is visiting us in the Land of the Seekers. Her name is D."

"Hello, D," said Tin.

"Hi," Dorothy said. An uncomfortable silence followed, so Dorothy, remembering instructions she received in etiquette class, determined to start a conversation by asking questions. "What are you reading?"

No Place Like Home

"It's a very big book with many pages," the Tin Man said proudly. "I'm an excellent reader."

He lifted the heavy book and held it for all to see.

Dorothy read its title aloud: *What You Need to Know about Everything.*

"Oh my," exclaimed Dorothy. "No wonder your book is so long."

The Tin Man nodded. "I'm only on page 2,876,150," he said. "Not even halfway. I have a long way to go."

"You must be very smart," said Dorothy.

"Oh, indeed I am," said the Tin Man. "I read more than anyone I know. I read studies, transcripts, articles, surveys, treatises, treaties, manifestos, outlines, platforms, and policy reports. I read prospectuses, planks, research papers, monographs, almanacs, and scientific articles. My favorite things to read are theses, term papers, conclusions, expositions, assessments, tracts, position papers, academic publications, inquiry reports, modern theories, and popular newspapers."

26

The Tin Man

"You must be brilliant."

"I am," agreed the Tin Man. He tapped a metal finger against his metal head. "There's no substitute for knowledge. It's what's in your head that counts."

"What about your heart?" asked Princess Holly.

"A heart is a hollow muscular organ that pumps blood through the circulatory system," said the Tin Man. "I read that in a book."

"Remember the book I gave you long ago?" asked Princess Holly. "It's called *The Book of Wonderful Words*. Where is it?"

"I'm sitting on it," said the Tin Man. "It makes an excellent chair." He stood and lifted the book to show Princess Holly. From the princess's skirt, a rainbow ribbon floated toward the book. The rainbow ribbon became rainbow fingers, which turned the pages.

"What does *The Book of Wonderful Words* say about hearts?" she asked.

The Tin Man began to read aloud, his eyes following the rainbow finger as it moved along the page. "The Forever King will change you from the inside out. Your heart of stone will become warm, loving and alive." (Paraphrased from Ezekiel 36:26.)

"Hmmm," said the Tin Man. "This book doesn't even mention the mitral valve or the aorta."

"Is it talking about a different kind of heart?" asked Dorothy.

"It must be," said the Tin Man. He continued reading, "With your transformed heart, you will trust me as your Forever Father. You will know me with your new heart." (Paraphrased from Jeremiah 24:7.)

"How can you know someone with your heart?" asked the Tin Man. "Seems to me the only way to know someone is with your head."

"Maybe not," said Dorothy. "I think I love my bird Tutu more with my heart than with my head."

"This is confusing," said the Tin Man. "Perhaps I need to check my other books for the answer."

"Who wrote your other books?" asked Princess Holly.

"Learned men and women from all over the world," he replied. "They come from the best universities and halls of learning. They are busy and important people."

"Busy doing what?" asked Dorothy.

"They are busy reading each other's books," said the Tin Man.

"Are they busy reading *The Book of Wonderful Words*?" asked Holly Sprite. "That book is the source of all wisdom. Remember that wisdom and knowledge can be two different things."

A puff of steam shot out of the Tin Man's funnel hat as he began to lose his temper.

"Do these wise men and women know Holly Sprite?" Harry asked, peeping out from behind Holly's gown.

"I don't know," said the Tin Man. "Does it matter? All this talk about hearts. I'm sick of it. It's head knowledge that counts." His metal mouth turned down into a frown as steam poured from his ears. "Knock on my chest," he said to Dorothy.

"Are you sure? That seems pretty rude."

"Go ahead. Knock on it."

Dorothy rapped her knuckles against the Tin Man's chest. "Ouch," she cried. "That's hard."

"Exactly," said the Tin Man. "Hard, just like it's supposed to be. After you knocked, what did you hear?"

"Nothing," said Dorothy. "It's hollow."

"Exactly again," he said.

There was silence for several moments as the little group looked from one to another. Without thinking, Dorothy and the two munchkins each placed a hand over their heart, reassured to feel the steady beat beneath their fingers. The Tin Man's arms hung at his sides, knowing that a search for signs of a heart would be useless. He tapped his head once again, stubbornly insisting, "It's what's in here that counts."

A breeze blew through the trees. The leaves seemed to whisper around them.

"How long have you been here?" asked Dorothy.

"A long time," answered the Tin Man.

"So you started searching for the Kingdom of Heaven, and then you stopped here?" she asked.

"Yes," he admitted. "I had to stop to read the books, the pamphlets, the treaties, the manifestos, the almanacs. The pile gets bigger every day."

The Tin Man

"Who brings you all of this reading material?" Princess Holly Sprite asked, with a knowing smile.

"Two crows," he said. "They must have a wonderful library. They even told me that at this rate, I may have more knowledge and book learning than any other creature in this entire country. In fact, they said that I deserve an award because of my incredible intellectual capacity. Obviously, those are two very wise crows."

Dorothy turned to the rainbow princess. "Are those the same two crows that tried to stop me from taking the narrow path?" she asked.

"Yes," said Princess Holly. "Fear and Chaos sent by Evileen. They will do anything to convince people to abandon their search for the Kingdom of Heaven. Evileen lets the crows know where a person is weak or insecure. Then the crows attack the vulnerable area. They attack with lies, with flattery, with distraction. Fear and Chaos. They are named well."

Dorothy turned to the Tin Man, with her hands on her hips. "If I were you, I'd leave this place and get back on the path," she said. "I'm seeking the Kingdom of Heaven. If I find it, I think it will answer a lot of questions that I have. Maybe it will answer some of your questions too. Heart questions. Not just head questions. Why are you just sitting here? Didn't Holly tell you about the kingdom?"

"Well, yes, she did," admitted the Tin Man. "It was quite some time ago. I heard about it. It sounded good, and I began the journey down the narrow path, but then those two crows came along, and we had a pretty interesting talk."

"I'll bet you did," muttered Dorothy.

The Tin Man shrugged his creaky shoulders. "Those two birds started talking to me, and they made a lot of sense. They told me that my journey wouldn't really get me anywhere, and that there isn't a Kingdom of Heaven. It's all a lie, so why bother? They sounded really smart. Every time I talked about stepping out on faith, they told me how faith is dumb. They said that if you can't prove something, then you shouldn't believe it. The Kingdom of Heaven? Well, it just started to sound so impossible, so I decided not to think with my heart, but to think with my brain. You should try it sometime."

No Place Like Home

Dorothy stepped forward and tapped a finger against the Tin Man's head. "Ouch. That's as hard as your chest. It sounds just as hollow too." She thought for a moment and then asked, "If you aren't traveling the narrow path seeking the Kingdom of Heaven, then are you switching to the wide path?"

"I honestly don't know," he said. "I mean, I've just been sitting here 'cause ... what's the point? I guess the wide path would be easier. Maybe I should take it."

"But doesn't it lead to destruction?" asked Dorothy.

"I don't know. Probably that's a lie too," he said. His arms jerked up and down as he talked. "I mean, seriously. Do you really believe that nonsense in *The Book of Wonderful Words*? Do you really believe there is some place—the kingdom—that is wonderful and eternal and you never die, and there is a way that leads to death and destruction? There's a kingdom in heaven and a kingdom on earth? I hate to be the one to break it to you, but evidence points to nothing beyond this place. Nothing at all."

Dorothy stared straight into Tin's shining, metal eyes. "So you are telling me you will sit here and not go anywhere? You won't search? You're cool with believing in the information brought to you by two birds named Fear and Chaos, but you can't believe that there is something beyond here, beyond all these books? Beyond this life? And you're not even curious about God's Kingdom on earth? What it is? Where it is? I thought you were supposed to be smart. Smart people are curious people. Smart people aren't afraid to change their views."

A puff of steam shot out of the Tin Man's metal hat. "It's not logical. What is this kingdom supposed to be, anyway? Where is it? I'm not exactly sure."

"Me neither," said Dorothy. "That's why I'm on this journey. That's why I chose the narrow path because it leads to the Kingdom of God. It's a quest, and I'm going to find out the truth. Why don't you come with me?"

"I don't know," said the Tin Man. "I'm pretty comfortable here."

He sat back down onto *The Book of Wonderful Words*. As he did, Dorothy heard his knees creaking. It was then that she noticed the

The Tin Man

scratches across his metal body and the dents in his legs and arms. Several tin patches were noticeable, inexpertly soldered upon his face. Lines of rust were visible at his shoulders and knees. The Tin Man looked as if he had been battered by a monstrous hailstorm. Would he be able to make the trip? Dorothy wondered. Could his creaking legs carry him over miles and miles of rocky paths? Was it possible that the Tin Man, the famous Tin Man, would not be a part of Dorothy's adventure?

CHAPTER 6

Rainbows and Righteousness

PRINCESS Holly Sprite stepped forward. "Hello, my old friend," she said, laying a hand on Tin's rusted shoulder. "Have hope. Don't give up. I've been with you all along. I let you choose the path and your timing. Today is the day for you to make a new choice. Remember, *The Book of Wonderful Words* says the kingdom is righteousness, peace, and joy in ... well ... me. For the kingdom of God is not a matter of eating and drinking, but of righteousness and peace and joy in the Holy Spirit." (Romans 14:17 NIV)

"Peace and joy," whispered Dorothy. "I could definitely use some of that. That's why I'm on this journey. That's why I chose the narrow path. Come with me, Tin. If Princess Holly says you can do it, then I know you can. What have you got to lose ... destruction?"

This time, puffs of steam shot from the Tin Man's ears. "I understand what peace and joy are," he said, "but what is this righteousness thing?"

The princess pulled a sprig of holly from her crown and tucked it into a metal seam just above where the Tin Man's heart would have been, if he had one. Instantly, new green leaves and red berries sprouted on her crown, filling the space from which she had plucked the sprig.

"Choose me and the narrow path, and you become new," she said. "You become perfect, without flaws or sin. You are perfect in the True King's sight."

"What?" exclaimed the Tin Man. "Look at me. I will never be perfect. Look at all the dents and scratches all over me. No, no, no; that path is not for me. I cannot be—what did you say? Righteous."

"I'm having a hard time with that one too, Holly," Dorothy admitted. "Can you explain?"

Rainbows and Righteousness

"Look at me," Princess Holly Sprite said. "What do you see?"

"Rainbows and light," shouted Dorothy.

"Smiles and love," said Tin.

"Your knees," said Pipkin.

"Your ankles," said Harry, not to be left out of the conversation.

"Watch me," said Princess Holly.

As they watched, narrow ribbons of rainbow revolved around Holly. Like slowly moving streamers, the colors circled her from head to toe, almost like hula hoops, Holly thought. One hundred hula hoops of every color, suspended in the air, slowly revolving around a radiant princess. The colors grew brighter and brighter until all color and shape were lost in perfect white light. The seekers knew that this was no ordinary light. This light was alive. It filled their heads with peace and joy so expansive that it seemed to push against the boundaries of their skulls. So much light. So much perfection.

"Is my head going to blow up?" asked the Tin Man.

The others wondered the same thing but didn't ask because peace, joy, and perfect truth filled them beyond words. The words of this world could not capture the truth of another greater world.

It lasted for just moments, this peek behind the physical world into a spiritual reality. Enlightenment. Shining truth. These were moments without words that revealed the Creator's perfect plan, the foundation of which was (and still is) goodness and love beyond comprehension. A perfect, perfect plan. They were all in the middle of it but hadn't known.

Then, suddenly, Holly appeared as her human form again. Princess Holly Sprite, crowned in green leaves and red berries, dressed in a gown of orbiting rainbows. As the physical world crept back into her consciousness, Dorothy found that she was kneeling on the ground, with her companions kneeling beside her.

"Oh … oh … oh," she said. "Light, love, joy. I wish I could feel that every day, all the time."

"Someday, you will," said Holly. "It's not for this time or this world."

"Somehow, right now, even this world seems perfect," said Dorothy. "There's a plan behind it all. I'll never be afraid again. I'll never be sad or lonely again, now that I know."

"Yes, you will," the princess said gently and a little sadly. "But it's only for a little while when it is measured against an eternity."

The munchkins and Tin Man pushed themselves up from their knees.

"Wow," said the Tin Man. "I totally forgot what we were talking about."

"Righteousness," said Princess Holly. "Perfection."

"Righteousness and perfection. That's what we just saw, isn't it?" asked Dorothy. "That's *you*?"

"Yes."

"We have to be like *you* to get into the Kingdom of Heaven after we die?" asked the Tin Man. "Perfect?" He looked down at the dents and scratches that covered his tin body and felt the patches on his face.

"Yes. Heaven is perfect. Nothing imperfect can live there."

"This is not good news," said Dorothy. "In fact, it's worse than every yucky thing that happened to me yesterday. I'll *never* be perfect."

"I know," said Princess Holly. "That's why I will give you my righteousness."

Dorothy, the Tin Man, and two munchkins all said the same thing at the same time: "Huh?"

"Do you love me?" asked Princess Holly.

"Of course," they all said together.

"Do you know that I love you? Do you want me to be with you forever?"

"Yes," they chimed in a chorus.

"Then this I give to you," she said. She reached a slender hand into her orbiting rainbows and pulled out a handful of streaming, multicolored light. It rested in her palm like a living orb.

Reaching forward, Princess Holly allowed the glimmering rainbow orb to roll off her fingertips. It floated for only a moment before it passed through Dorothy's shirt, her skin, her bones, her heart, and took root inside an inner secret place.

"Oh my," exclaimed the Tin Man. "Did that hurt?"

"I didn't feel a thing," said Dorothy. She placed her hands upon her chest and then on her stomach. "Is it still in there?" she asked.

Rainbows and Righteousness

"Always and forever," said Princess Holly. "That is my righteousness that I give to you. When my Father, the True King, the Forever Father, looks at you, he will see that you asked me to give you this gift, and I gave it to you. He will see you as righteous, as perfect."

"Are you sure he'll still know it's me?" asked Dorothy. "Won't your rainbows hide who I really am?"

"No," Princess Holly replied, laughing. "He knows exactly who you are."

"What about me?" asked the Tin Man.

"And me?" asked Pipken.

"And me?" asked Harry.

"Do you want me to be with you and in you forever?" asked the princess. "Do you want to be covered by my righteousness?"

"Yes!" they all shouted.

Reaching back into her swirling rainbow ribbons, Princess Holly Sprite took a handful of light and placed it into the chest of Tin, then Pipken, then Harry.

"You're in here?" asked Tin asked, rubbing his chest.

"Yes."

"And you're also out there, where we can see you?"

"Yes," said Holly. "For now, you can see me."

"This is a wonderful mystery," said Dorothy.

Princess Holly smiled and nodded.

"This requires a celebratory caper to mark and memorialize this propitious and fortunate occasion," said Pipken.

Harry began, "What my brother means is …"

"I know exactly what he means," shouted Dorothy. "Let's *dance!*"

Dorothy discoed, Tin Man tapped, Harry hustled, and Pipken polkaed.

Even Princess Holly hip-hopped, popping and locking as her rainbow skirts whirled in rhythm to the sound of celebration.

But when the travelers stopped dancing, Princess Holly was nowhere to be seen. There they stood in the deep, dark woods, surrounded by brambles and branches, looking down the path into the great unknown.

"She's still inside here, isn't she?" Dorothy asked, touching her heart.

"Yes," said the Tin Man. He tapped his chest with a metal finger, and although a sound of hollowness echoed back, he knew that he was no longer empty.

"You're coming with me to find God's Kingdom on earth, right?" asked Dorothy. "I think I understand the heavenly kingdom now. It's after we die, when we realize all the beautiful mysteries that we don't see now. But still, there's a kingdom here on earth, and that's the one I want to seek. You're coming, right, Tin?"

"Yes," the Tin Man said. "I'm tired of sitting around."

"Can you leave all your books and papers?" asked Dorothy.

"I guess I have to if I'm going to go anywhere," he said. He cast a wistful look around at the stacks, piles, and shelves of other people's opinions and conclusions. Then he glanced at the evergreen and berries, tucked into a seam of his chest, a reminder of the living, loving rainbow heart Holly had placed within his metal chest. "Let's go," he said.

"Can we come?" Harry asked excitedly.

Pipken added, "We would relish the opportunity to accompany you on your expedition to the Kingdom of God."

"I don't know," Dorothy said. "In the original story, the munchkins don't go on the journey." Then she remembered what Princess Holly had said: "This is your story. No one else has a story exactly like yours. Things will happen in their own way and time."

"Okay," said Dorothy. "Let's all go together."

The two munchkin brothers cheered.

"I'm ready to roll," said the Tin Man. He tucked *The Book of Wonderful Words* beneath one arm, his trusty axe beneath the other, and off they went into the deep, dark forest.

CHAPTER 7

The Book of Wonderful Words

IT is a regretful truth that even when we receive a wonderful gift, it is sometimes a very short time indeed before that gift loses its wonderfulness and seems quite ordinary. In fact, we often think about some gift we *haven't* received; it fills our thoughts and becomes an unfilled desire.

So it was with the Tin Man, whose rusty elbows and knees began to squeak most horribly after they had walked awhile. It was wrong of the others to laugh, but it is a sad fact that when one is tired or frightened, it becomes easier to laugh at the unintended noises made by other people's bodies.

"I'm not sure the righteous rainbow light is inside me at all," grumbled the Tin Man, raising his voice above the squeaking. "I can't see it or feel it. I don't believe in things I can't see." He stopped walking and folded his metal arms across his metal chest.

"Do you believe in the wind?" asked Dorothy.

"Of course I do," said Tin.

"Can you see it?"

"Well, no."

"How do you know it's there?" Dorothy asked.

"I see what it does," said Tin. "I feel it."

"That's right," answered Dorothy. "Just because you can't see that you are a new creation doesn't mean you aren't. In fact, when I first chose the narrow path, I didn't feel much at the beginning, but the more I listen to Holly and learn, the more I feel changed. I think I'm starting to get this righteousness thing. We're righteous in the Forever Father's eyes, even if we don't feel like we're righteous."

There came the sound of Dorothy's stomach growling. "Let's rest," she suggested. "Does anyone have anything to eat?"

"I don't need to eat anything," the Tin Man said, suddenly feeling better about his rusty joints since without a stomach, he had an area of superiority over the others. "Nope, not me. You all need to eat. But not me. I'm just fine."

"Must be nice," said Dorothy.

"I've got some gum fruit," said Harry. He pulled out a folded handkerchief, opened it, and revealed six bumpy purple fruits the size of boiled eggs. They smelled like pumpkin.

"What does it taste like?" asked Dorothy. One bite into the fruit answered that question. "Gum and wax," she said, wrinkling her nose. She continued to chew and chew and chew. There was the smell of pumpkin but not the taste. At last, she swallowed it with an audible and painful gulp. Pipken and Harry, on the other hand, popped one after another into their mouths with relish.

"Hey, Tin, as long as we're here, let's look at the next pages in *The Book of Wonderful Words.* You were reading about hearts, right?" asked Dorothy. "What else does it say about hearts?"

Tin picked up the book he had been carrying and turned the page. It said, "Trust in the King of Kings with all your heart, and do not depend upon your own limited understanding. Princess Holly Sprite will guide you. She will never turn away from you or forget you. She will be with you through sunshine and storms. She will help you to guard your heart against the lies and distractions of Evileen, Chaos, and Fear." (Paraphrased from Proverbs 3:5–6, Isaiah 41:1013, Philippians 4:7.)

"*The Book of Wonderful Words* is a good guide, isn't it?" asked Dorothy. She sat down on a hummock of moss and leaned back against a huge tree. "I'm glad we all are traveling together," she said. "Tin, you sat around for so long, reading your books but doing nothing. Now you're on the road to the kingdom. How does that feel?"

"Pretty good," Tin admitted. "I guess I can't just read about the kingdom without trying to find out where it actually is. I've got to

The Book of Wonderful Words

believe it and act on that belief," he declared. "I've spent too much time staying in one place. I'm ready. Let's get going. No more sitting around like mushrooms." He took a creaking step onto the yellow brick path. "Ready?"

No one answered, so Tin looked around to discover that the others, exhausted from all their walking, had fallen asleep. Even Dorothy snored just a bit as she lay upon the moss. Tin's spirits rose again as he discovered yet another point of superiority.

I don't have to rest or sleep, he told himself. *They have to eat. They have to rest. I don't.*

With nothing to do but wait for the others to awaken, Tin picked up the one and only gum fruit that had not been eaten. He took a tentative bite, wondering what it would be like to eat. He tasted nothing, so he studied the fruit more carefully, poking it with his metal-tipped finger. He considered how he had been squeaking badly mile after mile and recalled some of the more hurtful giggles from his companions. Then he took the fruit and rubbed it against his knee. Waxy scrapings peeled away and filled the spaces between the inner and outer rings of the ball bearings. He moved his knee back and forth, working the waxy substance into his joint. SQUEAK ... Squeak ... squeak ... squeak ... silence.

He performed the same routine on each joint: ankles, knees, hips, elbows, neck, knuckles. In no time at all, he was moving like a Swiss watch and sounding like a well-oiled door. He placed the unused portion of the gum fruit beneath his tin hat and waited for the others to wake up. When at last they did, they continued their journey refreshed. For a while, the Tin Man marched squeaklessly before them, proudly and silently leading the way as the merry travelers wondered at the aroma of pumpkin that surrounded them.

CHAPTER 8

Memories of Yesterday

THE narrow path wound its way through the forest. A canopy of trees filtered the sunlight above them as they passed a stream that burbled between two mossy banks. They picked berries along the way, eating so many that their lips turned purple. Nuts on the ground were plentiful and a snap to crack open, as the Tin Man could easily crush them between his metal fingers. The munchkins, great tree climbers, clambered up to pick the fruit in the upper branches. A particularly tasty fruit, which the munchkins called "junibees," grew in rubbery trees that bent beneath the weight of the little climbers. Junibees tasted like honey and oranges, supplying enough hydration to keep the travelers going when there was no water.

After a period of sunshine and plenty, they found themselves walking cautiously through a shaded stretch of path that wove through the trees. With each step, the forest grew more dense. Not a single ray of sunlight reached the forest floor. Around them came the strange sounds of unseen animals: growls, hissing, chattering. At times like this, the travelers would sing songs to reassure themselves. Dorothy found herself singing a happy song she had often heard her mother singing, an ancient song from 2015

It wasn't long before the munchkins had learned the chorus and sang along. The Tin Man yelled, "Nae, nae" and "whip whip," at the appropriate moments. The brave little group sang and marched over gnarled tree roots and beneath hanging moss.

The munchkins sang the Munchkin National Anthem, which extolled the beauties of the country and the courage of its little people. Like the people who lived there, the song was very short, as there are no words that rhyme with "munchkin."

Memories of Yesterday

After a while, the little group fell silent, trudging along through the dark, strange landscape. Dorothy found herself thinking about her mother, her father, and Chad. Where were they? What were they doing? Were they looking for her? Had they given up hope of ever finding her? How could she find her way back home if she didn't know where home was? What about Tutu? Was the little budgie in a lifeless heap beneath storm-ravaged rubble? Or was she flying around, lost, hungry, and frightened? In her mind, Dorothy could so clearly see Tutu's bright black eyes, the light blue cere above her beak, and two little blue cheek patches. Dorothy pictured how Tutu would sometimes ruffle her lime-green breast feathers and scratch beneath her wing with her long, pink toes.

"Sweet sweet," Tutu would say when Dorothy returned home from school. "What up? Toodle-oo." Then there was that eight-note medley she sang so often.

Dorothy's mind wandered to the image of Danny and Kimmy kissing beside the lockers. With memories, both good and bad, filling her thoughts, she wandered through a strange land, with even stranger companions.

Sometimes, when one has distance to cover and journey's end is both uncertain and unseen, the miles grow long. One foot after another. Over and over. Dorothy's neck ached from staring down at the path, choosing each footstep carefully in order to avoid potholes and roots. Her head filled with thoughts of Danny. Back home, if she still had a home, was the note he had written to her only last week. Folded and unfolded so many times, the creases were soft and fuzzy. She had memorized his words:

Dear D,

I don't know anyone like you. I never have. I never will.

I am so lucky to have you in my life. I can't imagine a future without you.

All my love, Danny

No Place Like Home

Of course, that note had been sent before the great betrayal. She reminded herself, it had meant nothing. Just penciled words on paper, lacking even the permanence of being written in ink.

Then there was Kimmy. Best friend. BFF. Hah. Dorothy's mind drifted to memories and loyalties that went as far back as preschool. To this day, she had never revealed to anyone the terrible secret that Kimmy had eaten crayons, up until third grade. Secrets shared and secrets kept. To her knowledge, Kimmy had never told anyone the true story of Dorothy expressing a desire to marry the purple Teletubby named Tinky Winky when she grew up. These were sacred trusts between friends who knew the worst and the best of each other.

But no more. Dorothy felt a heat rise within her, and her jaw grew rigid as she pondered the disloyalty of her closest male and female friend. Her stomach churned. Too many junibee fruits, or too many dark thoughts?

Where are you, Princess Holly Sprite? she asked herself. *My mind is spinning out of control. Help me.*

Like a wind behind storm clouds, the corrosive thoughts were pushed from her mind by new thoughts. Wonderful words of life took their place:

> Dear Dorothy, when your thoughts wander into darkness, pull them back into the light. Remind yourself of my presence. Think about goodness, virtue, courage, and beauty. Think about whatever fills you with joy. My perfect peace will pour into your heart." (Paraphrased from Philippians 4:8 and Isaiah 26:3.)

The image of a little green budgie head with blue cheeks popped into Dorothy's mind. "Sweet sweet," she whispered to herself, as she marched bravely forward into the unknown.

CHAPTER 9

Darkness, Doubts, and Division

"HOW many bricks do you think we've walked over?" asked Dorothy. They had traveled in silence for so long that she felt the need for conversation.

"A lot," said the Tin Man.

"That's true," said Dorothy.

"Exactly fifteen million, three hundred thousand, one hundred and twenty-six bricks," said Pipken.

"In addition to an extensive vocabulary, my brother memorized algebraic formulas at the Munchkin Academy of Extensive Knowledge," explained Harry. "I have no doubt that his algorithm is accurate. After all, my brother attended ..."

"The Munchkin Academy of Extensive Knowledge," groaned Dorothy. "I know. I know."

The Tin Man looked quizzically at Dorothy, noticing the change in her tone. As he was made of metal, not flesh and blood, he did not understand how tedious it can be to hear the same story over and over again. Nor did he know that it was algebra homework that led to the kiss shared between Danny and Kimmy.

"I'm so tired," said Dorothy.

"*Et participes te lassum*," said Pipken.

"That's Latin for 'I share your weariness,'" Harry explained.

"Well, then, why couldn't he just ... Oh well. Never mind." Dorothy was too tired and perhaps a little embarrassed from her earlier snarky comment to finish the sentence.

No Place Like Home

The travelers stepped off the path and wandered a ways to find a space between the trees, large enough for them to sit.

Sitting cross-legged on the ground, Dorothy said her feet hurt.

"I'm low on steam," Tin groaned. Two measly puffs of steam pushed their way from the top of his hat. Toot toot.

Pipken and Harry said nothing at all, as they were already fast asleep on the ground.

"I thought this was going to be easier," said Dorothy. She removed her green sneakers and began massaging her feet. She felt the air pressure change, as if a storm was imminent. Her shoulders sagged beneath an invisible weight. From the very depths of her chest came a long sigh. The branches above moved and then parted to allow a spinning funnel of brown cloud to settle on the party. With it came the smell of something vile and dead.

"Hello, my darlings," said Evileen, who floated down on her broomstick, two big crows perched on either shoulder. "Of course you're tired," she said sympathetically. "You chose the longest, hardest path."

"L-l-longest. H-h-hardest," crooned Fear.

Chaos added, "Each brick that paves the narrow path, each brick is just a lie. It leads to disappointment. You'll get there by-and-by. So when you reach the end of this and find there's nothing more, you'll know the truth was Evileen's. There's nothing past death's door."

Chaos launched himself from Evileen's shoulder, dragging a wing over the munchkins' faces as he landed on the ground. Harry and Pipken woke with shouts of alarm.

"Not to worry, my little men," Evileen said. "We come in peace. We heard your cries of pain, hunger, and weariness. We want to help."

"Really?" asked Harry.

"It doesn't feel good to be lost, does it?" said Evileen. She tried to smile sympathetically, but her pointy, sharpened teeth ruined the effect.

"You're l-l-lost," said Fear. "So very l-l-lost."

"We are?" asked Pipken. He nervously patted the braided beard that circled his waist.

"You mean this isn't the way to the kingdom?" asked Tin.

Darkness, Doubts, and Division

"There is no kingdom," said Evileen. "You don't believe all that noise about a loving God, do you? If God were so loving, would this path be so hard? I don't think so. Do you?"

Some of Tin's hinges and ball bearings were beginning to burn. "Maybe you're right," he grumbled. "It shouldn't be this hard."

"Let's go back," said Harry.

"Indubitably," Pipken agreed. "Our sojourn along an expansive, uniform boulevard would be more agreeable, would it not?"

"Of course it would," soothed Evileen. "When you get to the end of the wide path, you'll have a nice surprise. Plus you'll meet so many more friends on the wide path who would walk with you. You wouldn't be so alone.

"S-s-so alone," Fear said, sighing.

Chaos croaked, "Don't follow the light. Ignore Holly Sprite. Go with the crowd, who stand tall and proud. Walk together with pride on the path that is wide."

Dorothy jumped to her feet. "Hey, wait a minute, you guys. Don't listen to them. Remember what Holly said about them being liars? They're just trying to get us to take the wide path. Remember where that leads?"

"To Smithereens?" asked the Tin Man.

"To destruction," Dorothy insisted. "To pain, to suffering, to regret, to fear, to chaos." She looked angrily at the crows and at Evileen, who had spiders crawling up her red leggings.

"I don't know," said Tin. "It was a lot more comfortable sitting back there with my books and diplomas."

"But you weren't going anywhere." Dorothy turned pleading eyes to her friend. "You were just sitting still, reading books that contradict each other, books with no answers, not even searching for the Kingdom of God."

"Hey," the Tin Man protested, "I was reading important journals and texts written by important people who research important things. I think that's important."

"Y-y-yes. V-very important," said Fear.

No Place Like Home

Chaos whispered into the Tin Man's ear, "Don't listen to her. Her mind is so closed, while your mind is open. Your brain power grows. You're smarter than she is. You're one cut above. Don't listen to lies about God's perfect love."

"You're right," Tin said, nodding at Chaos. "I should be the one making decisions around here. I'm the smartest. I don't have to listen to other people when I am smarter than they are."

"But you got off of the path," insisted Dorothy. "You quit searching and believing. How smart was that? You weren't even looking for the Kingdom of God anymore. What could be more important than that?"

Evileen slipped an arm around Tin's shoulder and lowered her voice. "It's easier for her than it is for you," she whispered. "She doesn't have to carry around that heavy armor like you do. She doesn't rust. She doesn't dent. It's easy for her. It's hard for you. She doesn't understand that, does she?"

Suspicion and anger began to fill the Tin Man's hollow chest. "You're right," he said. "She doesn't weigh very much. I've got to lug all this metal around. It's not fair."

Chaos, still perched on Tin's shoulder, said, "You're made out of metal. You're meant to be hard. You're surrounded by softies. So be on your guard. What can they teach you? They're dumber than you. They only have lies. They haven't a clue."

"N-n-n-no clue," Fear said, with a shake of his head.

"What about these poor guys?" Evileen asked, turning to Pipken and Harry. "My little men, this traveling must be difficult for you. Aren't you hungry? Aren't you tired? Dorothy doesn't even care, does she? She's not a munchkin. She doesn't care about munchkins. She's never even liked munchkins."

"Our legs are short," the munchkins exclaimed. "We have to take twice as many steps as she does." They glared at Dorothy.

"Sh-sh-short legs," said Fear. "C-c-can't do it. T-t-time to leave the trail."

"Oh my. That's not fair, is it?" Evileen asked kindly. "It's easy for her. It's hard for you, my dear little men. Dorothy never thinks about your needs, does she?"

Darkness, Doubts, and Division

Chaos crooned, "She's different from you. She just doesn't care. You climb trees for her food, and you hang in the air. She's just using you till you fall in your graves. You're nothing to her, just two little slaves."

"Slaves. Servants. So sad, my little friends," said Evileen. She sat upon her broomstick, which hung horizontally in the air, her feet dangling just inches above the ground. Leaning forward, she pulled first Harry, then Pipken onto the broom to sit on either side. "Rest here," she said. "Feels good, doesn't it? Just floating like this? Rest yourselves. You deserve it. Want to go back? I can carry you."

"C-c-carry you. So-so tired." said Fear. He flew in lazy circles around the Tin Man's head. "Heavy metal. H-h-harder for you."

With each circle the crow flew, the Tin Man's eyes began to roll. He was no longer seeing or listening. Round and round and round, Fear flew.

"Oh no!" Dorothy yelled in alarm. "Tin, you're getting hypnotized. Don't listen to those crows and that witch. They're the ones who tried to get us to take the wide path. They lie and manipulate. Remember?"

Fear continued his airborne revolutions around Tin's head, repeating over and over, "D-don't r-remember ... d-don't r-remember ... N-never happened. N-never happened."

Round and round, the Tin Man's eyes rolled, seeing nothing.

In desperation, Dorothy picked up a rock from the ground. It was the size of her fist, and she hurled it at Fear to knock him out of his orbit. The stone missed the crow by barely an inch and whacked Tin on the shoulder, just above his holly sprig. With a loud *boom,* a deep dent appeared, and Tin's eyes stopped rolling.

"What's going on?" he asked.

Evileen began to laugh. So did the munchkins, who had been given yummy junibee tarts to eat. The tarts were so delicious that they didn't notice the spiders and centipedes crawling across their knees.

The Tin Man looked at his new dent and then frowned angrily at Dorothy.

"Holly," Dorothy yelled into the woods. "Princess Holly Sprite, I need you. "Help. Help."

No Place Like Home

Immediately, a glorious light appeared, eclipsing the witch and crows, who disappeared in a blaze of luminescence. In the presence of so much light, the darkness could not stay. Shadows fell away as Holly's light blazed. The munchkins fell from their broomstick perches onto the ground, landing on their round bottoms.

"Ooof," sighed Harry.

"Egads," cried Pipken.

Robes of living rainbows moved gently around Princess Holly as she took shape in her rainbow gown. "Hello, my beloveds! How may I be of service?"

"This narrow path leads to nowhere," grumbled Harry.

"I concur," said Pipken.

"It's not fair," the Tin Man said, inspecting the new dent in his shoulder. "D is throwing rocks at me. I'm heavier than she is, so it's harder for me to walk. It's harder to be made of metal than it is to be made of skin. Life was easier back with my books. I should have listened to myself and not to you and Dorothy."

"What does your book say?" asked Holly. "The one I gave you."

Tin Man looked around to find that he had left *The Book of Wonderful Words* in the dirt beside the brick path. As he picked it up, it fell open to a page, and he began to read:

"Trust me, the King of Kings. My words are your guide. An ocean cannot fit into a teacup. One day, you will understand the ocean of my love. For now, dear one, trust me and not your own limited understanding." (Paraphrased from Isaiah 55:8–9.)

"I don't get it," complained the Tin Man. "I read more books than anyone else. I'm the smartest one in this group. Why shouldn't I trust my own understanding?"

"*The Book of Wonderful Words* has the answer to that," said Princess Holly Sprite. "What does it say?"

Tin began to read again:

"'My understanding is not your understanding. Your methods are different from my methods,' says the Forever King. 'As a rainbow is above the earth, so are my goals above your goals and my knowledge is greater than your theories.'" (Paraphrased from Isaiah 55:8.)

Darkness, Doubts, and Division

"Don't listen to that awful book," Evileen chided. Her voice came from the air, although she remained invisible. "Lies, just lies. Trust your own way of thinking. You have every reason to be angry at Dorothy. All of you do. She's the one who got you into this mess."

"Evileen gives us tarts to eat," added Harry, "filled with junibees. D doesn't give us tarts. D's legs are longer, so it takes twice as much effort for us to cover the same distance as her. Sometimes, she's walking while we have to run. She makes us climb trees to get fruit for her. She treats us like servants. Our boots weren't made for walking. It's not fair. It's just not fair."

"*Non aequum*," Pipken agreed.

"D secretly hates munchkins," Harry said with a shake of his head.

"Not as much as she secretly hates people made out of metal," said the Tin Man.

"I don't hate anybody," Dorothy insisted. "Quit making stuff up."

"Now, Tin," said Princess Holly Sprite. "Think with that brain of yours. Feel with that new heart of flesh that you have. Do you really think that D is selfish? That she doesn't care about you? Has she tried to hurt you or help you? Hasn't she walked right by your side?"

"Well, yes," Tin admitted. "But … but … It's harder for me."

This time, when the words came out of his mouth, they sounded a bit silly. He considered that this land was his home, and the munchkins were his fellow countrymen. Dorothy, on the other hand, was in a strange place, far, far from home, with strange (to her) creatures. The many miles of traveling together had created a closeness. They had talked much of the way, and Tin had learned that Dorothy had lost her mother, her father, her brother, and her cherished little Tutu. He had learned that Dorothy's parents no longer loved each other and how she wished things were different. Hopes and sorrows shared during the long journey had strengthened the bond of their friendship.

"Aw, D," he said sheepishly. "I guess I wasn't really thinking."

"Oh, you were thinking all right," said Princess Holly. "It's *what* you were thinking that's the problem. Remember what we said about Evileen, Fear, and Chaos?"

"They're manipulative," Harry said, wiping the junibee jam from his mouth and looking abashed. "Wolves in sheep's clothing."

"Gold is the witch's fishhook," Pipken added thoughtfully. "Or in our case, perhaps it is being exhausted and yearning for junibee tarts."

Dorothy threw her arms around Tin. "Oh, Tin. If I didn't care about you, I wouldn't have asked you to come with me. I'm tired too, and I'm sorry if I sometimes get grumpy. But we're all in this together. We are all seeking the Kingdom of God on earth. We know about the Kingdom of Heaven because the princess told us about it, and *The Book of Wonderful Words* talks about it."

Harry remembered the moment when he had seen Princess Holly Sprite in all her heavenly glory. "The brightest light is truth," he said.

"Joy, peace, patience, goodness, faith," said Tin. "I've read about those things in *The Book of Wonderful Words*. It felt so good when I actually saw them come to life."

Princess Holly looked pleased. "Where did you see them come to life?" she asked.

"In you," said Tin.

"In you," the others agreed.

"There is no darkness in you," said Dorothy. "No fear, no chaos, no untruth."

"How did we get so confused?" Tin asked, addressing the munchkins.

"Let me guess," said Holly. "Did a couple of crows pay you a visit? Did they fill your head with fear and confusion? Did they offer you an easier way? Did they cause you to doubt your quest?"

"Yep," said Dorothy. "They did all those things."

"Did they turn you against each other?" asked Holly. "Were some of you feeling more important than others?"

With regret, the Tin Man recalled his claim to superior intelligence.

"Where there is strife, there is pride," said Princess Holly. "But wisdom is found in those who take advice."

Steam dribbled slowly from the corners of Tin's eyes. He wiped it quickly away with a handkerchief given to him by Pipken. "I'm sorry," Tin said. "Maybe I'm not as smart as I think I am."

Darkness, Doubts, and Division

Dorothy replied, "You know, Tin, I'm learning that people who think they're smarter than everyone else aren't smart at all. They close their eyes and ears to what anyone else has to say. If you're not seeing and not listening, how smart can you be?"

"Ouch," said Tin. He heaved a big sigh that rumbled through his chest like distant thunder.

Dorothy threw her arms around him as the munchkins hugged his ankles and knees.

"Don't worry, Tin," said Dorothy. "We're all in this together. And remember, you are righteous. Not perfect, but righteous. Right, Holly?"

Princess Holly Sprite blew a rainbow kiss to each one of them. Four kisses floated across to four cheeks; they landed, glowed for a moment, and then disappeared.

"Never listen to Fear and Chaos," she warned. "Those little stinkers will do anything to get you to stop seeking the kingdom. They take their orders from Evileen. She wants to make your life so miserable that you stop seeking. She wants you to argue with one another. She wants others to look at you and see how lost, confused, and angry you are. Her plan is for you to give up. To cause you to ..."

"Stay in one place forever?" asked Tin.

"Yes, my dear Tin," she said. "She will appeal to your pride. She will have you place the writings of ordinary men and women above *The Book of Wonderful Words*. In this way, she will trick you and lure you from the narrow path that leads to the Kingdom of God."

The Tin Man dusted off his book and tucked it protectively beneath his metal arm.

Holly broke four sprigs of berries and leaves from her crown. As before, new evergreen leaves and new berries immediately replaced the broken stems. She tucked one sprig into Dorothy's hair, one into each munchkin's cap, and one into the seam in the Tinman's chest, where it joined the other sprig he had received earlier. A surge of courage pulsed through each heart.

"Beloveds," Holly said lovingly, "remember that those crows and Evileen lie. There is no truth in them."

"To lie," said Harry: "an intentionally false statement."

No Place Like Home

Pipken added, "To deceive, fabricate, distort, misrepresent, perjure, fib, libel, cast aspersions."

Dorothy looked annoyed and was about to repeat her earlier words about fools who feel wise in their own eyes. However, a quick glance at Princess Holly stopped her from saying anything because, without saying a word, the princess let her know that Pipken was the first and only person in his munchkin family to graduate from the Munchkin Academy of Extensive Knowledge. When Pipken was a child, others made fun of him because his beard began to grow at three years old, instead of the usual forty years old. He also had seven toes on one foot, which meant that he must have his left boot specially altered. Consequently, he was not so quick to go wading in streams with other frolicking munchkins because of his fear of their cruel comments. With those things in his past, it was understandable why he took such pride in his diploma.

Dorothy saw Pipken with new eyes as he continued speaking: "... dishonesty, evasiveness, slander, perjury."

She and Princess Holly exchanged knowing smiles. "Wow," Dorothy said. "It's hard to ignore those crows sometimes. I gotta tell ya, sometimes, I feel hopeless."

"But you're not," Holly reassured her. "It's impossible to avoid those bad crows and their evil whisperings. Evileen is real, and she wants nothing more than to hurt and confuse you. D, you did the exact right thing when you called my name. There is beautiful power in my name. It brings hope and light. The crows and Evileen hate hope and light. They disappear when it surrounds them. As for you and Tin and Harry and Pipken? Even friends disagree and get cranky sometimes. That's where forgiveness comes in."

"Sorry about the rock, Tin," said Dorothy.

Tin's fingers tapped gingerly across the new indentation in his shoulder. "I don't mind," he said. "I was hypnotized. You were just trying to save me." He looked a bit proud. "This special scar will remind me not to get carried away by lies from my enemies. Give me some tin."

They high-fived.

"Down low," said the Tin Man. He low-fived the munchkins.

Darkness, Doubts, and Division

"Hey, Tin," said Dorothy. "Just so you know, that's a little old school. We fist bump now." She showed him how, and soon exploding fist bumps and laughter filled the air.

"All right, my beloveds," said Princess Holly Sprite. "Back to your travels. Remember, no one said it would be easy, but there is much joy along the way, and your quest is a good one. A righteous one. Help each other whenever you can. Encourage one another."

Each considered the glowing rainbow light that Holly had previously filled them with. They knew it would always be there, a piece of her and somehow all of her, in good times and bad, a marvelous mystery, which they hoped to understand better someday.

The sound of tinkling silver bells wafted through the air. They watched as Princess Holly began to twirl. Violet into indigo, into blue, into green, into yellow, into orange, into red, into silver. Like lightning revolving. A fountain of living light. Then she was gone.

"What a curious adventure we are having," said Harry.

"It is most singular," Pipken agreed. "What could possibly happen next?"

CHAPTER 10

The Scarecrow

AFTER a short walk along the narrow path, the Tin Man exclaimed, "Look." He pointed ahead to a spot on the path where dappled light lit the ground. "Sunshine." He began to run, the aroma of pumpkin trailing behind him. The others followed and soon found that they were out of the woods.

Miles of cornfields stretched ahead, the stocks green and tall, heavy with ears of corn ready for harvest.

"It looks like south Texas," said Dorothy.

"Is that near Smithereens?" asked the Tin Man.

"Maybe," said Dorothy. "They have a lot of tornadoes there. Hey, what's that?" She pointed to a scarecrow hanging from a post between rows of stalks. His burlap face smiled a faded red. Straw stuck out from beneath a lopsided hat. A long horizontal stick ran through his sleeves and across his shoulders, ending with a white gloved hand at either end. Dorothy thought he looked like a capital T with a head on top. His overalls reminded Dorothy of something a farmer would wear, and indeed, his overalls had once been worn by the farmer who tended these fields.

"Here you are," cried Dorothy. "At last."

"Who's that?" asked Scarecrow. His painted eyes gazed at the newcomers.

"I thought you would be first," said Dorothy.

"First?" asked Scarecrow. "First in what? First in line? First come, first served? First and foremost? First cousin? First impression?"

"Never mind," said Dorothy.

"First aid? First class? First dibs? First down? First light? First love?"

The Scarecrow

A vision of Danny popped into Dorothy's head. First love. First kiss. First betrayal.

"I ain't forgettin' nuthin', am I?" asked Scarecrow. "Yup, yup. Suspect I forgot. You see, I ain't got … I forgot."

"Wait," said Dorothy. "Let me guess. A brain?"

"Well, yeah. That's it." He twisted his head from side to side, straw scattering from his neck. "How did you know I ain't got a … uh … uh …"

"Brain," said Dorothy. "Long story. By the way, who told you that you don't have a brain? That seems a little harsh."

The Scarecrow thought for a moment. "Ummmm … Funny. Seems I cain't remember. Ya know why I cain't remember? It's cause I ain't got a …"

"Brain," said Dorothy. "We get it."

She looked around to find that the munchkin brothers were chasing each other through rows of corn. The Tin Man poked the Scarecrow's tummy with his metal finger.

"Not very substantial," he said. "A bit of a fire hazard, I would think."

"Ain't that the truth," answered Scarecrow. "I cain't be sure cause I ain't got a …"

"Good grief," exclaimed Dorothy. "Who told you that you don't have a brain? Could it be some crows? I'll bet they spend a lot of time in this cornfield. You know, big black birds that talk a lot?"

"Well, little missy, now that you mention it, I do remember them crows," said the Scarecrow. "They started out right friendly. Talkin' to me night and day, the way they done."

"I'll bet they did," said Dorothy.

"What did they talk about?" asked the Tin Man.

"Well, let me think on it a mite. Hmmm. Hmmm. I'm thinkin' they kept talkin' 'bout what's in my head. Or more likely, they talked about what's *not* in my head. Yup, that's it. They was sayin' that without a …uh…"

"Brain," supplied Dorothy.

No Place Like Home

"Right. Without a brain in my noggin, I ain't so good at thinkin'."

With a quick movement of his axe, the Tin Man chopped down the pole. The Scarecrow slid to the ground in a puff of dust. Tin and Dorothy helped him stand up, stuffing a few extra corn shucks into his clothing for good measure.

"Those crows are so evil," said Tin.

"No, sir, they really wasn't," said the Scarecrow. "They helped me to know how dumb I am. Nice fellas."

"Oh, Scarecrow," Dorothy said. She gave him a loving pat. "Those crows lied to you. That's what they do. You *do* have a brain."

"What? You mean it ain't just straw? Hmmm," he considered, tapping his head, thinking deeply. "Now that you mention it, there was that other one. The beautiful rainbow lady. She said my brain was workin' just fine."

"Princess Holly Sprite," exclaimed Dorothy.

"Yes'm, that's the one," said the Scarecrow. "She was walkin' right down this here brick road with me from the very start. Oooo-weee. She was a nice one. Sweet as molasses and bright as lightnin'. She never made me feel like them crows did. You know what that little gal told me?"

"What?" asked Dorothy.

The Scarecrow

"She done told me she knowed I had a brain 'cause she's the one that put it in me." He touched his head with a soft-gloved finger. "She said I was a new man and that she was givin' me a new heart too. I wonder if I still got it."

"You still do," Dorothy reassured him. "No one can ever take away your new heart."

"What if I lose it?" he asked.

"You can't," Dorothy assured.

"Well, that's a mighty good thing to know."

"Did she put a rainbow orb in you? A piece of herself? Did she say she'd always be with you?"

"By jingo, that's exactly what she said."

"Then what happened?" asked Dorothy.

"Well, we got this far," said the Scarecrow. "I told her I could take it from here. I mean how hard can it be? You just gotta follow them bricks, right?"

"There are lots of paths," the Tin Man warned.

"It's got to be the right one," added Dorothy.

"Hmmm," said the Scarecrow. "That ain't what them crows said."

"No doubt," said Dorothy. "Do you remember when you first asked Princess Holly to walk with you?"

"Sure. That was before I met them crows. We was in a big field with a sparkly green bench. My face was painted on fresh. That Princess Holly walked with me for miles. Sometimes, she even carried me. I kid you not. She's a strong little thang, even if she's made out of rainbows and light. Hey!" He looked surprised. "That was a smart thing for me to say."

"Yes, it was," Dorothy said, encouragingly. "Your brain works just fine. What you're missing is confidence, not a brain. What else did Princess Holly tell you?"

"Well, I'm a thinkin'. She said I can call on her any old time, and she'll hear me. That is 'zactly what she said. She says she gonna whisper truth and love in my heart and in my brain, the one that she done give me."

"Did you ever call on her?" asked Dorothy.

"Yeah, a couple a times." The Scarecrow made a rustling noise as he walked with Dorothy and Tin back toward the path.

"Did she help you?" asked Dorothy.

"Sometimes."

"Did you talk to her like friends talk?" she asked.

"Not really," said the Scarecrow. "Mostly I just asked her for stuff. Like a new pole to hep me stand straighter. New straw after a rain. A new hat too. A family of mice been livin' in my head for a while, and I think I need a little house cleanin' up there. It's a tad rank, or so I been told by some blue jays. Also, sometimes, I get sad or cold when it snows. I done asked her to change the weather."

"Did Princess Holly say you'd never be sad or wet or cold or smelly?" asked Dorothy.

"No," admitted Scarecrow. "She done told me she'd be my buddy and love me forever and ever and ever ... through sadness, rain, snow, and them bad smells. For sure, she promised me that things would get better."

"Did the crows promise you anything?" asked Dorothy.

Scarecrow gave a little hop. "They sure did," he said. "They said I'd be happy from mornin' to night, seven days a week, if I joined up with them. They done said I'd be the most popular scarecrow in the land and that peoples just gonna love me all the time. They told me my life was gonna be Easy Street from here on out. They hepped me see that all them wrong things in my life is caused by other folks, and I ain't to blame for none of it."

"Been there," the Tin Man said, sheepishly.

"Did the crows ever scare you?" asked Dorothy.

"Well, now that you mention it, after they told me how great I was, I started listening to them more and more. Then they started telling me how dumb I was and that my brain got eaten by them field mice. That was scary."

"Think about it," said Dorothy. "You were made to scare crows. They aren't supposed to scare you. Right?"

"Now that you mention it, it do seem a bit upside down," said the Scarecrow. "Don't nobody want field mice livin' in they head, I can tell you."

The Scarecrow

"They don't live in your head," said Dorothy. "That was a lie."

"I seems to remember Holly sayin' somethin' else, 'bout givin' me righteousness, peace, and joy."

"That's her job," said Dorothy. "What are you feeling right now?"

"Hope," said the Scarecrow.

"Yes, she gives that too," said Dorothy. "Hey, why don't you get back on the path again? Come with us."

"Where you goin'?" he asked.

"To find God's Kingdom here on earth," said Dorothy.

"That's where I was goin'," said the Scarecrow, "till them crows got to me. You know, I done seen other people walk by here. They kept a-goin', but I done stopped."

"You can always decide to start again," said Dorothy.

As the Scarecrow stepped one foot onto the path, two big crows came from nowhere, Fear settling on one flannel shoulder and Chaos on the other.

"Howdy," said Scarecrow. "You fellas done come back? I'm just gettin' ready to start back on that there narrow path that leads to the kingdom."

"L-l-l-long, h-h-h-hard walk," said Fear.

Chaos spoke next: "Perhaps you should think about other fun things, like baseball and ice cream and ruby red rings. There's football, spaghetti, and good things to eat, like cookies and pizza and hamburger meat."

"Mmmm," the Scarecrow said, stepping back off the path into the cornfield. "That sounds good, fellas. Where can I get a hamburger?"

Dorothy grabbed his arm. "Scarecrow, you don't eat, do you?"

The Scarecrow looked confused for a moment and then began to laugh. "By jingo, li'l gal, you're right. I don't eat. I ain't got no stomach. Just straw." He patted his belly. "So that there spaghetti and hamburger stuff ain't for me." He looked from Fear to Chaos and said, "Sorry, fellas. I'm a-gettin' back on that path."

"Shoo," cried Dorothy. She pushed Fear and then Chaos from the Scarecrow's shoulders. They screeched horribly while flying off into the forest.

No Place Like Home

"They're just trying to distract you," said Dorothy. "They want more than anything to get you off the right path. You've got to focus."

"What if them crows come back?" he asked.

"Resist the crows, and they will fly away from you," said Tin. "That's what *The Book of Wonderful Words* says." His swung his axe in the air to make his point.

"Princess Holly specializes in getting rid of lying crows," Dorothy added. "And that's why we travel together. We help each other. We encourage each other. It's easier to not get scared and give up when you're with friends traveling to the same place."

"Well, let's get a-goin'," cried Scarecrow.

He wrapped one arm around Dorothy's shoulders and the other around the Tin Man. The flannel felt soft against Dorothy's neck. The smell of clean straw on one side and the smell of pumpkin on the other reminded Dorothy that for the moment, she had a good friend on either side.

The Scarecrow picked up the same loving vibration. "I love y'all," he said. "I got the best friends in this world."

Dorothy wondered which world he was talking about. It didn't matter, though, because for now, they were all together, holding each other up.

She called over her shoulder, "Pipken! Harry!" Stalks of corn bent in a wave as the two munchkins scampered back.

"Hey, where them little'uns come from?" asked the Scarecrow.

"They're with us," said Dorothy.

"Are we leaving the corn forest now?" asked Harry. "Are we off to find the kingdom?"

"Yes, we're off," cried Dorothy. "Nothing's gonna stop us."

From many miles away, a purple-faced witch in red leggings gazed into her crystal ball, watching the band of hopeful travelers. "That's what *you* think, my little darling," she croaked. She rubbed her claw-tipped fingers together. "Next time, we will destroy you, utterly and completely. You're as good as dead."

CHAPTER 11

The Lion

THEY left the open country, clear skies, and cornfields behind and soon found themselves, once again, in a dense forest, surrounded by branches, vines, and the strange sounds of unseen creatures. Thick foliage above blocked out any hint of sunshine. Crablike creatures scuttled across the path, the sound of their pincers rattling like tiny swords.

They came to a large bramble vine entwined around a tree, twisting up and up until it branched into a giant bugle flower the size of a basketball. Its pretty rose color and fragrant smell were delightful.

"Oh my," said Dorothy. "How lovely."

She stepped from the path to admire the enormous blossom. Stretching on tiptoe, she breathed in the floral-scented air. As her face moved closer to the flower, there came a sudden movement behind her. Eight pairs of arms pulled her backward just as the flower's bell closed with a snap. It opened again to show rows of tiny savage teeth.

The Tin Man swung his mighty axe at the base of the bramble, slicing it in two. The flower screamed and shriveled immediately into a blood-red, wilted mass.

Dorothy was frightened but not hurt, as she had stumbled back into the Scarecrow who had, obligingly, fallen onto the ground to cushion the young girl's fall.

"What in the world," she exclaimed, her breath coming in great heaving gulps.

"You have narrowly escaped the deadly fate of the *Caput flos manducans*," Pipken declared.

"Head-eating flower," explained Harry.

"What?" cried Dorothy. "Head-eating flower? But it was so beautiful, and it smelled wonderful."

"It's not so beautiful once it eats your head," said the Tin Man. He helped both Dorothy and the Scarecrow to their feet.

"Oh my," said Dorothy. "I must be more careful." She brushed the dirt from her jeans and stood still for a moment, waiting for her quick-beating heart to slow down.

"How can something so lovely be so dangerous?" she asked. Then she remembered Princess Holly's words about evil sometimes disguising itself.

"Ooo-weee," said the Scarecrow. "That was a close call, little miss. You don't wanna be stickin' yor head in them plants no more."

That sounded like an excellent idea to Dorothy. She helped Scarecrow rearrange his straw.

"Put a little more in my biceps," he said. "I got a feelin' I'm gonna need some extra muscle on this here trip."

"Stay on the narrow path," Tin warned Dorothy. He wiped his axe on the grass, ridding it of the flower's scarlet toxins.

The Lion

"I didn't know flowers could scream," said Dorothy.

"As a general rule, they don't," explained Scarecrow, "but sometimes, general rules ain't so general."

It was at this point that Pipken and Harry pulled ears of corn from their pockets.

"Perhaps some light refreshment is in order," said Pipken.

"I don't eat," said the Scarecrow.

"Do you sleep or get tired?" asked the Tin Man.

"Nope," he said.

Dorothy knew that the Tin Man was pondering the loss of his bragging rights. No longer was he the only one in the group who could walk endlessly without sleep or food. In an effort to encourage him, she took an ear of corn and asked him to cut it into smaller pieces with his axe. He was happy to do so and happier still when he saw Dorothy enjoying the corn.

Dorothy and the munchkins snacked on corn and continued their trek through the forest. Twigs snapped beneath their feet. Another sound became clear, a rustling in the underbrush around them. Was something or someone moving?

No Place Like Home

They had the feeling they were being watched and followed, but the forest was so thick they couldn't see what it might be. Then suddenly, without warning, a massive figure appeared beside them. It was a lion, who roared and sprang onto the path, its cavernous mouth baring sharp teeth. With a growl, it bounded toward Dorothy. She cocked her leg and swept it forward, her green sneaker punching the lion's nose in a roundhouse kick that would have broken a board.

"Owww," cried the lion. He sat on his haunches as the others watched tears streaming from his eyes. "What did you do that for?"

"Dude," said Dorothy, "what did you expect? I take kickboxing. You tried to scare the wrong chick."

The lion rubbed at his nose with a mighty paw. "Is it bleeding?" he asked. "Is it swelling? Do you think I need stitches?"

"You big baby," said Dorothy.

"I am not a big baby," he said, crying.

"I know exactly who you are," said Dorothy. "You're the Cowardly Lion."

"Who told you that?" asked the lion. "Was it the mice? The squirrels? Are you going to kick me again?" He continued to cry.

"Get it together, dude," said the Tin Man. "You're afraid of everything."

"Am not," sniffled the lion.

"I didn't notice any profiles in courage when a little girl dropkicked you." Tin held the axe behind his back so that he wouldn't frighten the lion further.

In an effort to calm the lion, Harry picked a flower (of the non-head-eating variety) and offered it to him.

"Get it away. Get it away," cried the lion, shrinking back. "Is there a bee in it?"

"Of course not," said Dorothy. She took the yellow flower and twined it into the lion's mane. "There," she said, patting it into place. "That looks nice."

"What if I'm allergic?" asked the lion.

The Lion

"Oh my word," the Scarecrow said, gently. "We ain't gonna hurt you. You just gotta quit growlin' and jumpin' and tryin' to scare the tar out of us."

"Did I scare you?" the lion asked, hopefully.

"Yes," said Dorothy. "For a nanosecond, you scared us."

That was good enough for the Cowardly Lion. He looked very pleased with himself and lay down on the ground. "Awesome," he said. "My friends will be so proud. That's what we do, you know. Frighten the other animals that live in the forest."

"Seriously? That's what you do?" asked Dorothy.

"We scare the squirrels and chipmunks," the Lion said proudly. "We scare all the little things. I'm bigger than just about any other animal around here."

"You're big and strong, but you're still a coward?" asked Dorothy.

"Well, sure, but the others don't know that. I hang out with the meanest animals, and since I'm the biggest one, the little ones think I'm mean too." The lion shook his tangled mane. "Since I run with all the other predators, everyone thinks I'm tough. When they see me coming, the small animals skedaddle as fast as they can. I hang out with a bunch of scary guys, and everyone else thinks I'm scary too. It's a pretty good deal."

"Do you feel joy and peace?" asked Dorothy.

"Are you happy here?" asked Tin.

"Hmmm," the Cowardly Lion said. "Not really, now that you mention it." He used a curved claw to pick at his teeth. "I used to have these great dreams about reaching the Kingdom of God."

"That's where we're going," shouted Harry and Pipken.

"Really?" asked the Lion. "I was on my way. Nothing could stop me. Thunderstorms? I kept walking. Nothing to eat? I kept walking. Skunks in a bad mood? I kept walking. Then I got to this place here and found out that I could be king of the jungle. Well, king of the squirrels and chipmunks. I guess that's what I was really meant to be. I made buddies with a bunch of other predators here. We hang out, and we're pretty much in control of this whole part of the jungle."

No Place Like Home

"Hold up," Dorothy said. "You got this far on the narrow path and then you decided to stop here?"

"That's right," said the lion. He shook his mane lightly so that he could smell the fragrance of the yellow flower.

"Oh no," said Dorothy. "Let me guess. Was it some crows who convinced you to stop here?"

The Cowardly Lion turned his golden eyes to Dorothy. "How did you know?" he asked. "They said that this was the best place for me, and they introduced me to all the other tough guys. It feels good to be part of a group."

"Fear and Chaos. They strike again," said Tin.

"Them crows ain't nuthin' but trouble," said the Scarecrow. "They told me I got field mice in my head."

"Mice?" cried the lion. "I'm afraid of them."

"Were you always afraid of mice?" asked Dorothy.

The lion thought back to his earlier years. "No," he said. "I can remember a time when I wasn't afraid of anything. That was before..."

"You met the crows and left the path," finished Dorothy. "The crows will give you thoughts that make you afraid and make you confused. Evileen sends the crows to stop you from seeking the Kingdom of God.

"What other junk did the crows tell you?" she asked.

The lion swung his head so that his mane moved, and he could see the yellow flower that Dorothy had placed there. It was clear to Dorothy that he liked the flower very much; she was glad that such a little thing could bring joy to her new friend.

"The crows told me that if I stay here, I can be part of a group. I can blend with the biggest, meanest animals, and all the little animals will think I'm not afraid of anything. Seriously, my best friends are tigers and wild pigs. You should see the little ones scatter when me and my buddies come around and start tearing things up."

"Are you happy here?" Tin asked again. "Do you feel peace and joy?"

"Not really," the Cowardly Lion admitted. "Sometimes, it's all right, but a lot of the time, I feel afraid. I don't know why."

Tin turned to a page in *The Book of Wonderful Words* and began to read. "It says here, 'Don't be afraid, my Dear One. I am with you. Don't

The Lion

give up. I will give you strength. You are in my hands. I am holding you next to my heart. What I say is true. Don't be afraid.'" (Paraphrased from Deuteronomy 31:6–8.)

"That's very encouraging," said the lion.

Dorothy patted the lion on his big, soft nose where her shoe had made contact. "Did Fear and Chaos also say you don't have enough courage to keep going? Is that why you stopped here?"

"That's exactly what they said," said the lion. "It's true. I'm too cowardly to seek the kingdom."

"Do you know what the crows are really good at?" asked Dorothy.

With one voice, the munchkins, Scarecrow, Tin, and Dorothy shouted, "Lying!"

"Them crows sure as shootin' ain't tellin' you the truth, pardner," said the Scarecrow. "They done told each of us tons of lies to get us off this here path."

"They told me that smart people don't search for the kingdom because it doesn't exist," said Tin. "Total lie. They said I was too smart to look for the kingdom."

"They done told me I was too dumb to look for the kingdom," said the Scarecrow. "They showed me lots of other fun stuff I could be doin'. Like talkin' to crows. Talkin' to blue jays. Watchin' the rain fall. Watchin' corn grow. There's lots more to life than just lookin' for the kingdom. They done told me that over and over."

"They told me it's easier to get to places if I ride on a broomstick instead of walking," said Harry. "Problem is, I don't want to go where that broomstick is headed."

"They disseminated misinformation about junibee tarts being more valuable than the integrity of true friendship," said Pipken. "That falsehood nearly interrupted my sojourn."

Dorothy nodded. "Princess Holly said the kingdom is filled with love, joy, and peace. Evileen tried to scare all of us into stopping our search for the Kingdom of God. She will confuse and frighten and lie to you. She'll find your weak points and use them against you."

"And offer you junibee tarts," said Pipken.

"So why don't you come with us?" asked Dorothy.

"Yes," added Tin. "We will help each other along the way."

"I'll climb trees and pick fruits and nuts for you if you get hungry," offered Harry.

"I will put flowers in your mane and kiss your nose," said Dorothy.

"My flannel shirt is very soft," said the Scarecrow. "You can lay your head to rest on me if you want to."

"I will teach you five-syllable words from my extensive lexicon," said Pipken.

"You wouldn't be embarrassed to be seen with a Cowardly Lion?" The lion's big golden eyes looked from one to the next. "I mean, I wouldn't want to walk down the narrow path with a Cowardly Lion. Would you?"

"Sometimes, we forget how powerful the names are that we call ourselves," said Dorothy. "Even if we just say them in our heads: Dumb, Cowardly, Failure, Weak, Ugly, Fat, Useless. Those aren't real names. Those are lies. You need a new name, mister."

"A new name?" asked the Lion.

"I'm changing your name," said Dorothy. "Right now." She tapped her finger on her chin, thinking. "Hmmm. What's another word for brave?"

"Valiant," shouted Pipken. "It means brave, bold, and determined."

"Perfect," said Dorothy. "From now on you are the Valiant Lion."

"Really? That's my new name?" said the mighty beast. "The Valiant Lion. I like that." He began walking proudly in a circle around the little group. Muscles rippled beneath his tawny hide. "The Valiant Lion, TLV, that's my name," he told himself. "That's me. I'm courageous. I'm the most valiant guy around. But wait a minute. What about my buddies? The tigers and wild pigs? If I get back on the narrow path, I'll have to leave them behind."

"They can come too," said Dorothy.

"Ha," said TVL. "You don't know them. They'd eat all of you up in two minutes. They'd turn the Scarecrow into a bed of straw and use the Tin Man as a container for raw meat. There's no way they will want to look for the Kingdom of God."

The Lion

"That's their choice. Maybe you need some new friends," said Dorothy. "Hey, Tin. What does it say about friends in *The Book of Wonderful Words*?"

Tin opened the book and began reading: "Wise friends will support you, encourage you, help you, and bring you wisdom. A bad friend will lead you down the wrong path and would rather see you fail than succeed in life. You must be brave enough to know when a friendship is leading you away from Princess Holly Sprite and our Forever Father. Ask Holly Sprite to help you choose good friends." (Paraphrased from Proverbs 13:20.)

"Interesting," mused TVL. "Is that book saying that it takes courage to leave behind bad friends? It would be valiant to walk away from the life I've been leading?"

"Sounds like it," said Dorothy.

TVL growled just a little bit. "But what will my old friends think of me?"

"Who cares?" asked Dorothy.

"I do," the Lion admitted. The Tin Man handed him a handkerchief, and the Lion blew his nose so loudly that two junibee fruits fell to the ground from a branch overhead. Pipken was quick to grab them.

Dorothy patted TVL's side. "Think about it," she said. "You'll be giving up a dangerous life. The animals you call friends are bullies. They only pick on the animals who are weak and little. What happens when you become old and slow? Will your friends turn on you?"

The Lion breathed in the sweet scent of the yellow flower in his mane. "I'm tired of being afraid of my friends," he admitted.

"Come with us," said Dorothy. "We are searching for the Kingdom of God. Princess Holly Sprite is with us all the time, even if we can't see her. We can talk to her. *The Book of Wonderful Words* has so many answers, answers about an invisible world, about our true Forever Father, who is the King of Kings."

"Is that like being king of the jungle?" asked the lion.

"It's much better," said Tin. "You have to growl and fight to be king of the jungle. The King of Kings is pure love."

"He doesn't fight?" asked the lion.

No Place Like Home

"He can when he wants to," said Tin. "But he would rather not."

"Peace and joy," said Harry. "That's what we're searching for."

"However, you must be warned about our adversaries," added Pipken.

"Yes," said Harry. "They are pure evil and would like nothing more than to stop us. A witch and two crows. There's no end to their cruel tricks."

"Don't mess with me, crows. I'm the Valiant Lion." TVL growled such a huge growl that the tree branches shivered, and animals miles away thought they felt an earthquake. "Oops," he said, placing a big paw over his mouth. "I didn't scare anyone, did I?"

"No," they all said.

"Good," said the Lion. He combed his claws through his mane and looked at the yellow flower again. "Every time I look at this flower, I will think about courage and valor. The valor to face what I must face. The courage to walk away from old friends and an old way of life."

"Every time I look at the big dent in my shoulder, the one from the rock that Dorothy threw, I will think about how I should not listen to the lies of Fear and Chaos," said Tin. "I will not turn away from the narrow path because the crows start filling my metal head with thoughts about how I'm smarter than everyone else and how only a dummy would trust *The Book of Wonderful Words*."

"Now that's what I'm talkin' about," said Dorothy. "Confidence. That's what we need. Knowing that Princess Holly Sprite is both in us and near us gives us the confidence and the courage we need to keep traveling down this narrow path. Am I right?"

They all cheered.

"Come on," said Dorothy. "Let's kick it up a notch. We're getting closer to the kingdom. I can feel it. Let's go."

"First, I must say goodbye to all my friends," said TVL.

"Seriously?" asked Dorothy. "You have to say goodbye to tigers and wild pigs, whose biggest goal in life is to scare and hurt little animals?"

"Well, when you put it that way," he said. He shook his mane thoughtfully.

The Lion

The Scarecrow held up a floppy gloved hand. "Maybe I ain't the sharpest tool in the shed," he said, "but seems to me that if yer gonna git back on this here path to the kingdom, you might best leave them bad fellers behind. Git a new start."

"I agree with my flannel friend," said the Tin Man. "It's like books. Sometimes, if we get caught in a bad chapter, it's best to just turn the page and start a new one. Don't look back."

"Maybe you can use your size and your muscles for something else besides scaring bunnies," said Harry.

"In point of fact," added Pipken, "I am finding the transportation options on this journey to be sadly lacking."

He winked at the lion, who understood the hint; he knelt down on the ground and said, "Climb aboard."

The strong arms of the Tin Man lifted Dorothy, then Harry, then Pipken onto the lion's broad back. TVL rose to his feet. The riders felt his muscles and tendons ripple beneath the tawny skin as he took his first steps onto the narrow brick path. Without a look back, the six travelers continued their search for the mysterious Kingdom of Heaven on earth.

"Ninety million, four hundred thousand, three hundred and two. Not counting the broken ones," said Pipken.

"Huh?" asked TVL.

"Bricks," explained Dorothy. "That's how many bricks we've walked over. Pipken keeps count. He is a really smart guy. He graduated from the Munchkin Academy of Extensive Knowledge." She smiled at Pipken, who blushed.

CHAPTER 12

Friends to the Rescue

IT was an odd group indeed who continued along the narrow path: a young girl in jeans and emerald-green sneakers, a dented and scratched man made of metal, a scarecrow with no discernible knees or elbows, two bearded men no taller than fire hydrants, and a lion with a scraped nose from where Dorothy kicked him.

Mile after mile brought them into different terrain. Sometimes, the path was smooth and sunny. Sometimes, the path became lost in shadow and storm. Throughout it all, the adventurers encouraged each other and felt great joy in knowing that they traveled together. When doubts and fear began to invade their thoughts (which always happens on such a journey), they called upon Princess Holly Sprite to replace their gloom with thoughts of light and truth. Sometimes, when the path ran directly up a steep hill, Tin would open *The Book of Wonderful Words* and read encouraging passages aloud until the group was ready to begin the climb.

Passing through a field of weeds, Scarecrow noticed that one of his sleeves was almost empty, the straw having fallen out along the way. The group stopped, climbed down from the Lion, and began to search for soft weeds to stuff into the Scarecrow's shirt.

Familiar squawking filled their ears, and they looked overhead to see Fear and Chaos flying above them in lazy circles.

"Uh-oh," said Dorothy.

Friends to the Rescue

The crows descended and landed atop a nearby bush. Addressing Scarecrow, Fear said, "T-t-t-tired. Y-you m-must be s-so t-t-tired."

Next came the rhyming words from Chaos: "I think you should rest now. It would feel so nice, to lie down, close your eyes, dream of sugar and spice. Your straw makes a pillow. You'll soon be asleep. In no time at all, you'll be counting sheep."

Scarecrow yawned, patting his mouth with a gloved hand from his one remaining arm. "Now that you mention it, I am a bit tired, fellas," he said. He sat down and stretched out on the path.

"No," Dorothy cried, pulling him to his feet. "You can't stop here."

"You're a scarecrow," the Tin Man reminded him. "You don't need to sleep."

"That's right," said Scarecrow. "I forgot. I don't even know how to sleep." He stood up, brushing the dust from his overalls.

Chaos flew to a nearby tree and whistled to get the Scarecrow's attention.

No Place Like Home

"Well, hey there, little fella," said Scarecrow. "You still here? Whatcha doin' up there?"

Chaos called loudly, "You look so bendy, with no bones to break, no muscles, no tendons, with never an ache. Can you climb this tree to the very tip-top? Your soft straw will cushion your fall if you drop."

"Well," said Scarecrow, "just as soon as I get this here arm fixed, I can give it a try. I ain't never climbed a tree before, but it might be fun to try."

"According to my calculations, we have only two more hours of daylight," said Pipken. "Perhaps we should continue our sojourn."

"That's right," said Dorothy. "Don't listen to them, Scarecrow. They're just trying to distract you from where we're going. We don't have time right now to climb trees."

"Yup, yup," said the Scarecrow. "Follow the yellow brick road, right?"

"Right," they all cried.

With his empty sleeve repacked with weeds, Scarecrow joined the group as they began their walk. Above them, the crows continued to fly.

"I wish they'd go away," said Dorothy. "Evileen must have told them to keep bothering us."

"They appear to be targeting the weakest link," said Harry, with a nod toward Scarecrow.

"He does have a hard time focusing on our mission," Dorothy admitted. She saw that the sun was setting, and not much light was left in the day to show their way.

She glanced at the Scarecrow and was dismayed to find that Chaos had landed on his shoulder with a new invitation:

"Searching for mushrooms can be so much fun. You might find a hundred. You might find just one. It's just like a game that you play in the park, and since you're a scarecrow, you can see in the dark."

"Now that does sound like a whole lotta fun," said Scarecrow. "I'll bet they's some fine mushrooms growin' in this here field." He stepped

Friends to the Rescue

off the path. "I can put the mushrooms in my hat," he said, removing it from his burlap head.

"No," insisted Dorothy. She pulled him back onto the yellow bricks and shouted to the others, "Help me, y'all. The crows keep distracting him."

The little group jumped into action, the Tin Man swinging his axe at the crows while the Lion gave a mighty roar. Harry jumped in an effort to catch the crows, while Pipken sacrificed his precious junibees, as he threw them at the evil birds.

Squawking angrily, Chaos and Fear flew away.

"Resist them, and they will fly away from you," Dorothy reminded them. She remembered the wise saying from *The Book of Wonderful Words*.

"Thanks," said Scarecrow. "Sometimes my mind gets a mite fluttery, and I can't focus."

"That's okay," said Dorothy. "That's what we're here for, and that's why we travel together." She took one of Scarecrow's soft hands in hers. The Tin Man took the other hand, and the six travelers walked a bit farther before they stopped for the night. They wanted to rest before the next day's adventure.

CHAPTER 13

Where Are We?

THE sun rose and set again and again, as the travelers pushed on. They shared food and helped each other through swamps and over shifting sand, while striving to react mildly to each other's annoying habits. When Fear and Chaos threatened them with discouragement, they read to each other from *The Book of Wonderful Words* and called out to Princess Holly Sprite.

When Tin's knees began to squeak, Harry and Pipken climbed the tallest trees in search of the waxy gum fruit for Dorothy and Scarecrow to rub into his metal joints. The nuts they found were easily crushed between Tin's powerful fingers, providing nourishment for those who needed it. When their feet hurt, the Valiant Lion carried them on his strong back. The talents of each, given willingly and joyfully, contributed to the well-being of the entire group. One morning, as they walked and talked, Dorothy suddenly stopped.

"Look," she cried, pointing. In the distance, they all saw a movement of rainbow-colored light.

"We're here," Dorothy cried. "This is it. The Kingdom of God on earth. We found it!"

"Let's go," roared TVL. The mighty lion galloped over the ground, his powerful legs churning the dust.

Dorothy clung to his mane for dear life. Pipken held onto Dorothy's waist, and Harry held onto Pipken. The Tin Man held fast to the Lion's tail, looking down at the ground as he was pulled along through the air.

In Dorothy's mind, she thought, *Goodbye, Yellow Brick Road. Goodbye, deep, dark forest. Goodbye, head-eating flowers. Goodbye, hunger. Goodbye, doubt. Goodbye, Chaos. Goodbye, Fear.*

Where Are We?

With miles and miles behind them, they broke into the sunlight and came to a halt in the middle of an open field. Wildflowers grew here and there among the grass. In the center of the field glittered an emerald bench.

"What?" Dorothy cried, as she slid down from the lion's back.

The two munchkins landed beside her.

"Hmmm. This looks familiar," said Scarecrow.

"I've been here before," added Tin. "I'm confused."

Gazing at his yellow flower, the Lion muttered to himself, "Courage, courage, courage. Be valiant."

"Isn't this where we started?" asked Dorothy. Disappointment dragged at the corners of her mouth.

"Hello, my beloveds." In a whirl of rainbow light, Princess Holly Sprite appeared.

"What's happening?" cried Dorothy. "We've traveled so far. We're back at the beginning. Why aren't we at the kingdom?"

"Oh, but you are." Princess Holly's silver hair gleamed beneath the green leaves and red berries of her crown.

"Maybe I ain't that smart," said Scarecrow, "but this looks a lot like Munchkinland to me. See, look at all them cute little fellas." He waved a floppy hand at the little people approaching from the forest.

"I don't get it," said Dorothy. "Is this some kind of joke?"

A sound of mocking laughter filled the air. A brown funnel cloud spewing noxious fumes descended into their midst. From the whirling dark confusion stepped an orange-eyed witch, wearing a tattered dress and red leggings.

"Oh my," she cackled. "You should see the looks on your faces."

"Y-y-your f-faces," cackled Fear, who perched on the witch's left shoulder.

Chaos added his verses of discouragement: "What were you thinking? Have you no remorse? The Wonderful Words just steered you off course. Why listen to Holly? She's not even real. Evileen's the master to whom you must kneel."

"Y-y-you're b-back at the b-b-beginning," cackled Fear.

No Place Like Home

The crows dilated their eyes and flapped their black wings. The grape-sized wart on the end of Evileen's purple nose pulsed with laughter.

An angry puff of steam shot out of the Tin Man's nostrils. "We're back where we started?" he asked.

"Oh, little Tin-Tin, I'm afraid you've been tricked." Evileen wiped a cobweb from her eyes. "This is rich. You poor little idiots. Are you disappointed? Frustrated? Tired? Did Holly Sprite promise you all this peace and joy hooey and not come through? I'm so, so sorry, but you have to admit I warned you, didn't I?" A spider ran from her chin up into her nostril. Fear watched it hungrily.

She continued with a big sigh, "Some things are just not meant to be. Finding the kingdom is hopeless, don't you know? There is no kingdom. It's all just a big fairy tale. How can you find something that doesn't exist? Holly knows that. She should have told you, that meany goody two-shoes. Oh, but my sweets. It's not too late to give up this tiresome trip and come with me."

"N-n-not t-too late," echoed Fear.

Tin turned to Princess Holly Sprite. "I thought we were seeking a Kingdom," he said. "But we've ended up at the very same place where we started. What's happening?"

Holly stood quietly and watched the scene unfold.

Evileen smiled, her pointed teeth glittering in the sunlight. "Oh, you little fools. You've all been bamboozled."

"I feel no bamboozle," said the Scarecrow. "Uh, what's a bamboozle?"

"It means you've been tricked," said Evileen.

"Beguiled," Pipken said, sadly. "Bluffed, burned, deceived, deluded, faked out, fooled, hoaxed, hoodwinked, snookered."

"Hornswoggled?" asked Scarecrow.

"Exactly," said Evileen.

"This is the very same place that I started," complained the Lion. "I left my great old life and my awesome gang to come back to the very beginning?"

"TVL, they weren't all that awesome," Dorothy reminded him. "Remember, you were afraid of your friends and just pretended to be like them."

Where Are We?

Steam puffed from Tin's ears. "Hey, Holly, I thought we were going somewhere new, not in a circle. What's the deal?"

Chaos, who knew exactly how to get beneath the Tin Man's metal, chided him for not rejecting the journey: "Your head, not your heart, should guide all your ways. No such thing as truth. No good God to praise. Believe all your own thoughts, and trust your own mind. You're smarter than they are, so leave them behind."

Tin looked around at his fellow travelers, wondering if he should have abandoned them and the narrow path long ago.

Next, Chaos flew to the Scarecrow and recited into his painted ear, "There's more fun to life than just walking along. There's dancing and cartwheels and singing a song."

"Come to think of it, that sounds like a pretty good idea," Scarecrow replied.

"No," cried Dorothy. "The crows are just trying to distract you."

Next, Chaos flew to the lion, who didn't even bother to shake the crow from his head.

Staring dejectedly at the ground, TVL listened as Chaos recited, "Remember when you and your friends were all kings? You chased and you frightened all small, furry things. The little ones ran when they saw you come near. You had their respect out of panic and fear. Old habits are better. They fit like old shoes, familiar and comfortable, just like old crews. Don't forget Growler and Slasher and Bully, those great friends of yours who were wild and so wooly."

"We had some good times," said the Lion. "Those guys really knew how to fight."

"Wait a minute," Dorothy cried, stopping. "Hang on, everybody. Let's talk. Think about it. Why do the crows and Evileen keep attacking us and trying to stop us on our journey? Why? There must be something they don't want us to find. They wouldn't be trying to stop us from seeking if there wasn't something to seek, right?"

"S-something to s-seek," mimicked Fear.

"Shut your beak, you bird brain," shrieked Evileen. "You're only supposed to repeat what *I* say."

"Sh-sh-shut it. B-b-bird b-b-brain." Fear rolled his beady eyes. Evileen cast a disapproving eye at both crows.

"You know, D," Tin said, "you're right." He touched the big dent on his shoulder that reminded him of the time Dorothy stopped him from being hypnotized by the lying crows.

"If there ain't nuthin' to find, then why is they workin' so hard to stop us from findin' it?" asked Scarecrow. "It's kinda like they knows there's somethin' there."

"That's genius, Scarecrow," responded Tin. "You're right. Holly never said we would actually end up at a place. She said that the Kingdom of Heaven is righteousness, peace, and joy. She gave us the righteousness when we asked her to be our guide. Remember when she put that rainbow light in us? She and the King of Kings can see it, even if nobody else can. That's our righteousness. I might have dents and scratches on the outside, and I know I'll make mistakes. But since Holly gave me the gift of righteousness, that's how our Forever Father sees me. That's how he sees all of us. He sees us as being perfect, like Holly is perfect."

"What about peace and joy?" asked Evileen. "You've been fighting with each other every bit of the way. You call that peace?"

"We didn't fight every bit of the way," said Harry. "Just sometimes."

"I corroborate that viewpoint," added Pipken.

Evileen turned to the Scarecrow. "Had any great thoughts lately with your moldy brain?"

"Well, yes'm," he said. "I been thinkin' bout how I learned to have peace even after them mean creepy crows whispered them lies in my ears. I think on Holly and the gift she done give me. I think on how *The Book of Wonderful Words* tells me how much the Forever King loves me. I think about my new buddies here. Right there, that give me some peace, and it feels swell. Seems to me maybe I should keep on this here narrow path and stop gettin' distracted."

"What about you, you big hairy coward?" Evileen turned to the Lion. She was now screaming so loudly that beetles and centipedes were

Where Are We?

traveling southward down her body as quickly as possible to escape the region of her mouth. "You sniveling, gutless poor excuse for a lion."

TVL placed his big paws over his ears and said, "La-la-la-la-la. I have a new name. It's the Valiant Lion." He looked the witch straight in the eyes and said, "You just don't get it, do you? It took courage to leave my old life, to leave my bad friends, to step out of my comfort zone, which is what I did when I got back onto the narrow path. You can be scared and still have courage. Frankly, I'm surprised you don't know that." TVL sniffed the fragrant scent of his yellow flower.

The munchkins began to laugh.

"Score," exclaimed Dorothy.

Evileen pointed a long, boney finger at the young girl. She tried to make her voice sound sympathetic. "You, my little darling. Did you get your boyfriend back? Didn't you lose your best friend? What is it about *you* that made them betray you, hmmm? Not good enough for Danny? Not pretty enough? Not smart enough to pick a better BFF? Even your little bird left you. You can't even keep your pet." She smiled her wicked smile with her pointed teeth. Dorothy felt her heart falter. It was true. Every bit of it. No best friend. No boyfriend. No Tutu. After all, maybe she was the most rejected person in the world. It certainly felt that way.

Tin Man, Scarecrow, Harry, and Pipken watched Dorothy as she stood there staring at the ground, at the green sneakers that had carried her across so many miles. Even the crows said nothing as they all waited, surrounded by silence.

CHAPTER 14

Truth and Lies

"I will never turn away from you. I will always love you, forever and ever, through sunshine and storms."

Wonderful words of truth flowed from the eternal spirit of Princess Holly and filled Dorothy's heart with the knowledge that there was a perfect plan underlying all of life.

"What is it about you that made them betray you, hmmm?" Evileen asked again.

"They betrayed me," Dorothy admitted. "It's true. That hurt. It still does. But it doesn't crush me. I understand that people will disappoint me sometimes." Dorothy looked into Evileen's orange eyes and placed a hand over her heart. "I have someone I can talk to about all that junk. She's always with me. She tells me what the King of Kings wants me to hear. She always loves me, in spite of anything that goes on. It feels good to know that whatever happens, wherever I am, I am loved completely by the Creator of rainbows and parakeets. It says in *The Book of Wonderful Words*, 'I will never leave you or forget you. I have always loved you. I will always love you, forever and ever, through sunshine and storms.' The King of Kings says, 'My love for you is constant. You can count on me and my love, always and forever.'" (Paraphrased from Deuteronomy 31:6 and Joshua 1:5.)

"Stop." Evileen clapped her hands over her ears. She shook her left shoulder, launching Fear into the air; he flew over to sit on TVL's head.

Fear whispered, "Y-you'll never be b-brave."

Truth and Lies

"Lies!" roared the Valiant Lion. With a sweep of his mighty paw, he knocked Fear off his head, causing him to tumble through the air and land at Evileen's feet.

Evileen shrugged her other shoulder, which sent Chaos swooping over to the Scarecrow.

Chaos perched on Scarecrow's flannel shoulder and began a lilting tune: "I like to daydream. I'll bet you do too. Pretend you're a camel, a goose, or a gnu. Let your mind wander freely from diamond to pearl. Think of this. Think of that. Hey, look. There's a squirrel."

At one time, the Scarecrow's head would have swiveled wildly, looking for a squirrel in a tree. However, this time, his painted eyes looked straight ahead, as he quoted from *The Book of Wonderful Words*: "We must pay close attention to what we have heard from Princess Holly Sprite, so that we do not wander away from her true and perfect words." (Paraphrased from Luke 11:28 and James 1:25.)

He looked at Princess Holly and added, "When my thinkin' stays on you, it feels all gentle in my noggin. I will keep a-goin' on this here path."

Their eyes connected, and Scarecrow felt peace and joy flow from his burlap head to his battered boots. He swept Chaos from his shoulder, surprised to find that the big crow was not as heavy as he had suspected. "I ain't afraid of no low-down, lyin' crows," said the Scarecrow, "when I got a princess and the King of Kings on my side."

Chaos saw the anger building in Evileen's purple face and knew that she was blaming him for his inability to bully the travelers. If crows sweat, he would have been sweating profusely.

He turned his venom on Pipken, saying, "I've seen your foot when you take off your boot. Those two extra toes are really a hoot. No wonder you don't wade and splash with a friend. One look at your feet would signal the end. A circus is where you could show off those toes. You'd bring in more gawkers than all the sideshows."

"Two extra toes?" asked the Tin Man. "I had no idea."

"Two extra toes?" echoed the Scarecrow. "Well, I'll be hornswoggled."

No Place Like Home

For once, Pipken was at a loss for words, ashamed as he was about his secret deformity.

Fear, sensing Pipken's sorrow, sprang into action, flying to perch on his pointed hat. "R-remember all the p-p-pain f-from y-your ch-ch-childhood? The other m-munchkins laughed at you because of your b-b-beard and your t-t-two extra t-t-oes. What kind of God would allow you to s-s-suffer like that?"

Pipken moved one foot in the dust to cover the boot patch that had been added to accommodate his extra toes. Then, changing his mind, he widened his stance and stood tall (for a munchkin). "Suffering? That is an accurate assessment of my youth," he admitted. "However, I suspect that in the long run, it has made me a more compassionate person. I am able to empathize with the unfortunate conditions of others. I comprehend, perhaps more than others, that physical imperfections have nought to do with one's character. Thanks to the encouragement of my friends and the truth I've learned from *The Book of Wonderful Words*, I am at peace with my past and also with my present physical imperfections."

"Physical imperfections?" asked Tin. "Get a load of these dents and scratches. Don't worry, Pipken. We've all got our flaws."

Harry, who silently watched the crows verbally attacking each of his friends, looked frightened. As he twirled the tip of his beard nervously between his fingers, he knew he was the next target.

Chaos landed on one shoulder, Fear on the other. "D-did you g-go to the Munchkin Academy of Ex-ex-extensive Knowledge?" asked Fear. "Are you as s-s-smart as y-your b-brother?"

Chaos chanted, "Just look at your brother. Seems he got the brains. In spite of your shortness, you have growing pains. You'll never be taller or smarter or bolder. You need a stepladder to cry on my shoulder. Did you go to college? Did you go to school? Compared to your brother, you're only a fool. He got a diploma. He made the grade, while all that you got was to stand in his shade."

Harry said not a word.

Truth and Lies

"P-p-p-pipken is the smart one. You're the d-d-d-dumb one," said Fear. "H-his b-beard is l-longer than y-yours. Y-y-you're sh-shorter than h-he is."

Harry stood silently, not blinking.

Fear continued, "D-d-d-didn't go to the A-academy, d-did you? D-didn't m-make g-good g-grades. Repeated third g-grade t-two times. You l-liked that girl L-lulu, who n-never even l-looked at y-you, d-did she?"

The munchkin said nothing, staring silently ahead.

The crows looked at each other, shrugged their wings, and returned to Evileen's shoulders.

"He's at peace," said Dorothy. "You can't bother him."

Evileen screeched, "You wretched, wretched creatures." The broomstick trembled in her hand.

Still, Princess Holly stood watching nearby. Without speaking aloud, she sent confidence and courage into the heart of each seeker. They heard her, even if it wasn't with their ears.

At last, the Scarecrow broke the silence. "I'm still confounded," he said. "Why are we here? We end up at the beginning? It don't make no sense. What changed?"

"*We* did," said Dorothy. "Okay, this is what I think. I think that the kingdom is in us, so it goes everywhere we go. If we listen to Princess Holly Sprite when she talks to our hearts, and if we study *The Book of Wonderful Words*, we will feel peace and joy in all situations. Good and bad."

"What about pain?" asked the Lion. "Will we still feel it?"

"Yeah," said Dorothy. "We can't escape that. People do mean things, and that's gonna hurt. Crummy stuff happens, like my house getting blown away by a tornado and me losing my favorite pet and my friends disappointing me, and my parents getting a divorce, but we get through it. It doesn't destroy us. Do you know why?"

"Why?" asked Pipken.

Harry still said nothing. He just watched.

"Because we know that we're not alone," said Dorothy. "In the middle of a storm, our Heavenly Father is with us. In the ups and downs of ordinary life, we have Holly Sprite, who lives inside of us. She speaks with the same voice as our Heavenly Father. She speaks to our hidden heart, a secret internal receptor that we don't quite understand. Sometimes, we think we can't hear her. But if we read from *The Book of Wonderful Words*, and if we truly seek her, her voice becomes more and more clear.

"There's something beyond this life," she continued. "It's the Kingdom of Heaven, where we will go one day. Heaven, where it will be perfect. There's no crying there. No pain. No meanness. It's perfect, and nothing imperfect can live there. That's why we need to be perfect. But since that's impossible, we ask Princess Holly Sprite to cover for us. She loves us so much that she gives us her very own righteousness, her perfection, to cover us in her rainbow light. That's for the Kingdom of Heaven that's not in this world. But we don't go there until we die."

"I don't want to die," said Tin.

"Me neither," said the Lion.

"Exactly," Dorothy agreed. "So for now, we try to live like we're in the kingdom. We do our best to love other people, to stand up to bullies. When we know how much we are loved, when we know that Princess Holly and our Heavenly Father watch us and care about us, every second of every day, it's possible to feel peace. I mean, seriously, does anything feel better than knowing that you are perfectly, completely, absolutely loved by the Creator of everything? Doesn't it just fill you with …"

"Love," said Tin.

"Peace," said Scarecrow.

"Joy," said TVL.

"Forgiveness," said Pipken.

Harry still said nothing, and it was at this point that the others became concerned. All except for Tin, who walked up to Harry and pulled a wad of pumpkin-scented wax out from each of the munchkin's ears.

"Whew," said Harry. "I couldn't hear a thing. Thanks, Tin."

"My pleasure, friend," Tin said, putting the wad of gum fruit back under his hat.

Truth and Lies

Fear and Chaos began to squawk. Evileen gave them such a look that they immediately shut their beaks.

"Love, peace, joy, patience, forgiveness," said Dorothy. "We will have those things in the Kingdom of Heaven. We can have those things here on earth if we stay on the narrow path, not perfect like heaven, but still wonderful. Bad stuff happens. Like when that flower tried to eat my head off."

"*Caput flos manducans*," said Pipken.

"Right," said Dorothy. "I almost got my head bitten off, but you guys saved me. That's what we'll do. We'll help each other through the hard times."

"We ain't never givin' up," said the Scarecrow. "No, sirree."

"See?" said Dorothy. "We might be back in this same field, but we're not the same people. We're not looking for a place that's different. It's we who are different. I know I am. We know things we didn't know before we started seeking. We learned things about life and truth and a reality that we don't see yet, at least not with our eyes. I learned lots of things on this trip. Like not to get angry if someone brags about the same thing over and over and to understand that there might be a reason why they do it." She glanced at Pipken, who had no idea what she was talking about.

TVL shook his shaggy mane. The yellow flower moved with his great head. "You're right, D. You know what? I learned that it takes courage to walk away from an old lifestyle, old friends, and old habits that keep me away from God. I learned that the Forever King has given me Princess Holly Sprite to be my Forever Friend. I can have peace even when things are hard, even when crows lie and call me a fraidy cat. From now on, when I hear those lies, I'm going to face them and roar-r-r-r-r."

All the munchkins gathered more closely around Princess Holly. She calmed them with a reassuring smile.

"That's the truth," said Scarecrow. "Just tell them lyin' old crows to shut up their big yappy beaks. Then you keep movin' on in a brave, happy way. You a Valentine Lion now."

"Valiant," the Lion corrected him.

"That's what I said: a Valentine Lion. Those crows ain't nuthin' compared to who I got on my side." He waved a floppy gloved hand at Holly.

Dorothy clapped her hands and said, "Yay! Y'all are getting it. We learned that we are a new creation once we decide to follow the narrow path and put our hope in the righteousness of Princess Holly Sprite."

"That's right," said Tin. "D, it's all because of your courage and determination. Thank you for taking us on the path with you."

"It's Holly who got me started," said Dorothy. "She's the one who showed me the way."

"I love you guys," said Scarecrow.

"Same here, brother," said the Tin Man.

"I owe all of you a lot," said TVL.

"I am indebted to each of you for your benevolence and generosity." Pipken removed his hat and made a sweeping bow.

"Ditto," said Harry.

"I think I'm going to puke," said Evileen. "Too much ooey-gooey love around here. My blood sugar is rising. My ankles are swelling." Indeed, Evileen's red leggings, like sausage skins, appeared to be on the verge of exploding. "I'll leave you for now. Fear? Chaos? Come," she ordered.

Evileen hopped aboard her broomstick, a crow perched on either shoulder. She rose into the air, leaving a powerful stench behind her. "You haven't smelled the last of me yet," she warned.

Chaos raised his wings in a threatening gesture and called, "When you least expect it, when your day is bright, we'll turn your sunshine into night. The peace you seek does not exist. It disappears like a foggy mist. The lies we tell you will sound true. We'll tell you what you cannot do. We'll tell you who you cannot be. We'll blind you so you cannot see. We'll tell you where you cannot go and all the things you'll never know. We'll move you to a path that's wide. Then Evileen will be your guide."

"Aw, baloney," said Harry.

The others began to laugh; Dorothy couldn't be sure, but Evileen appeared to turn a darker shade of purple.

Truth and Lies

"W-w-we w-w-will r-r-return," crowed Fear.

"Perhaps I could refer you to a speech pathologist to work with you on that articulation disorder," suggested Pipken.

"W-w-w-w-w-w-w-w-w-what?"

"Do you have a hearing problem as well?" asked Pipken.

"We aren't afraid of you," roared the Lion. He balled his paws into fists, posed in a fighting stance, and growled, "Bring it on."

"Hey," yelled Scarecrow. "Don't think you can addle our brains no more. We knows what you bad birds is up to. We got Princess Holly on our side. You ain't nuthin' but a buncha feathers compared to her."

"That's right," shouted Tin. His voice echoed through his chest and boomed up into the sky. "That's right. We have righteousness, peace, and joy. Nothing's stronger than that because it comes from the King of Kings and Princess Holly Sprite."

Dorothy shook her fist into the air. "Get out of here, Evileen, with your dirty birds," she yelled. "Go eat some bugs."

Evileen and her partners in wickedness rose higher and higher into the sky, finally disappearing into a brown cloud.

"All right, boys," said Dorothy. "High five."

"Old school," said Tin. "Let's fist bump."

"You're a fast learner," Dorothy said. A girl's hand, two smaller hands, a floppy gloved hand, metal fingers, and a giant lion's paw bumped each other and exploded into a burst of rainbow colors. Violet, indigo, blue, green, yellow, orange, and red.

"Congratulations, my beloveds," said Princess Holly Sprite. "You have learned well. D, you found what you were seeking. It's time to head back."

"What?" cried Dorothy. "I'm not ready. I haven't even had time to say ..."

"Goodbye. Goodbye. Goodbye," came a chorus of voices, growing more and more faint as the sound of wind grew louder.

"Wait," cried Dorothy. She felt herself enveloped in a funnel of rainbow shadows. Around and around she swirled in a cocoon of light and color.

CHAPTER 15

Home and the Kingdom

DOROTHY'S eyes flickered open. She was sitting scrunched up in a closet beneath the stairs with her brother, Ross, and Jay. She could feel Chad's flannel sleeve pressed against her arm.

"Dude," said Chad. "What just happened?"

"Is it over?" Jay asked, his voice shaking.

"Let's check it out," Ross said, opening the closet door. "In Dr. Spencer's book on tornadoes, he says that after a tornado, one should listen to local news and weather stations to find out what's going on. Also, I wrote a paper once on the danger of power lines going down during a tornado. If you guys read as much as I do and had my IQ, you'd already know this stuff."

Dorothy gave Ross a funny look as if she had just had a déjà vu moment. *He thinks he knows everything,* she thought to herself. *Just like, just like ... no, it couldn't be. Or could it?*

"Are we still alive?" asked Jay. "That was super scary. I thought we were going to die."

He's so big, and still he's the most afraid of any of us, Dorothy thought. *Just like TVL. Strange.*

Jay shook his shaggy hair out of his eyes, his massive chest breathing a sigh of relief. His big body seemed to take up most of the space in the closet. One after the other, they each crawled out.

The three boys sat down on a living room couch that had moved to the other side of the living room. Viewing the destruction, they were alarmed to see that the front window was smashed and lay across the living room floor in thousands of pieces. Broken glass, leaves, papers,

Home and the Kingdom

and books were scattered everywhere. Lamps were toppled over, shades crushed, their light bulbs smashed. Chad shivered in the breeze that came from the kitchen through a doorway that no longer held a door. Dorothy stood in the middle of the room, a smile slowly spreading across her face.

"I just don't get it," Chad said when he saw his sister's grin. "Dot, I thought you'd be in pieces after everything that just happened. Look at this place. It's destroyed."

"How are you so chill over there?" Jay asked. "I thought I was going to have a heart attack."

"Courage, my friend," said Dorothy. "You need a little courage. Honestly, I'm feeling sort of peaceful. Even in the midst of this storm."

"Midst?" Ross repeated. "Did your sister just say 'midst'?"

"Huh?" asked Chad. "I don't know. Did she? Maybe. I don't know. I wasn't paying attention. You know, maybe she got a concussion. Or she's in shock. Or I'm in shock. Or maybe …"

"Focus, Chad," Ross said.

"I found the kingdom," Dorothy proclaimed. "The Kingdom on earth. It's right here." She touched her heart. "And here." She touched her eyes. "I guess I'm just seeing things differently since I was in the Land of the Seekers. I learned that you can have peace, even when things are going wrong. You can feel joy, no matter what, because you understand that you're never alone. The Forever King, our God, created everything and controls everything. Yeah, there are witches and evil crows and mean people and tornadoes. That part of life stinks. I'm not gonna lie. But if you choose good friends, they'll save you from wicked head-eating flowers. They'll share their junibees with you."

"Junibees?" The boys looked puzzled.

"I'm serious," said Dorothy. "Knowing God and talking with Princess Holly Sprite reminds me how much I'm loved."

"Did you get hit on the head?" Chad walked to Dorothy to see if he could see any injuries. "Seriously, sis, you're starting to worry me." As he moved across the littered floor, he felt scratchiness inside his flannel shirt.

No Place Like Home

"What's this?" he asked. "Talk about weird. I've got hay or weeds or something in my shirt. The wind must have blown it there." He shook it out onto the floor.

"That's straw, not hay," said Dorothy.

"I'm allergic to straw, dude," said Jay. He began coughing so loudly that it came out like a roar-r-r-r.

The others looked at him. "You sound like you belong in a zoo, bro," Ross replied.

"This is crazy. My brain hurts," Chad complained. "What's going on?"

Eight little notes whistled from outside the window that was no longer there. Eight little notes that Dorothy would have recognized anywhere.

"Do-ray-me-fa-so-la-ti-do!"

Dorothy turned and raised her hand into the air. Through the broken front window flew 2.2 ounces of green feathers with two little blue cheek patches. Pink claws curled around Dorothy's finger as the parakeet landed.

"Tutu," she cried. "Where have you been? I thought you were lost forever or hurt or …"

"What up?" asked Tutu. The little budgie sidled up Dorothy's arm to sit on her shoulder. Once there, she cocked her head and chirped into Dorothy's ear, "Sweet sweet."

"Oh, Tutu!" cried Dorothy. "I was so afraid you were gone. I thought maybe you …"

"What's in her beak?" asked Chad.

Dorothy looked closely, recognized the floral scent, and found that Tutu was holding onto a yellow flower. "Oh my word. It's the Lion's flower. Tutu, how did you get it? Were you there all the time? Were you in the other world with me?"

Home and the Kingdom

Dorothy took the flower from Tutu's beak and held it up for the boys to see. "This flower stands for courage," she said. "Courage in the middle of tornadoes, evil crows, witches, and flowers that bite your head off. Harry gave this flower to the Lion."

Eyes darted from side to side as the boys looked at each other. No words were necessary. Chad circled his finger beside his ear in the universal sign for cuckoo.

With her beloved green parakeet on her shoulder, Dorothy looked at the surrounding destruction. She remembered the loving words of Holly Sprite: "I will never turn away from you. I will always love you, forever and ever, through sunshine and storms."

The sound of footsteps came from the kitchen. Then came the anxious voice of Dorothy's mother: "Dot! Chad! Boys! I'm home. Are you okay? Where are you? Oh my goodness. Look at this house. Are you okay?"

"We're all right," Chad called back. "But you'd better talk to Dorothy. I think maybe she got hit on the head. Maybe even a couple of times."

"I'm fine, Mom," Dorothy called. "Everything's cool. My head is just fine."

Mrs. K. hurried into the living room, scanning the destruction and breathing a sigh of relief at seeing that her children and their friends were safe.

"What happened here?" she asked.

Dorothy turned to the boys and her mother. She said, "I found what I was looking for, Mom. I found what *you're* looking for, too, but y'all just don't know it yet."

Her mother, Chad, Jay, and Ross stared in bewildered silence.

"Don't worry," said Dorothy. "I'll explain it to you later."

With Tutu firmly perched on her shoulder, she walked to the broken window and looked out.

"Hey," she cried. "There's a rainbow. That's a good sign. Get ready for an adventure, everyone. I'm taking all of you with me next time." She turned and tossed the yellow flower to the boys. "You keep this, my friends," she said. "Courage. You're gonna need it."

"Concussion," Chad whispered to his mother.

Dorothy, who knew better, calmly picked her path through the surrounding wreckage, her heart filled with peace and joy at the knowledge that a King and a Princess would always be with her. Always and forever.

As she left the room, Tutu turned her little head, puffed out her blue cheeks, and called, "Toodle-oo."

For perhaps the first time ever, the boys didn't laugh.

AFTERWORD

Jessie had been studying the Kingdom of Heaven and the parable of the sower for a year before she wrote the play *No Place Like Home*. The 2017 play for Stand Ministries had as its theme the parable of the sower, found in Matthew 13:1–9. She prayed before writing her play but couldn't decide how to make the story more relevant with interesting characters. As she prayed over the play, she recalls the Lord giving her a vision of *The Wizard of Oz* characters representing each type of soil.

She realized the Tin Man could represent the "hard ground," where the seed didn't take root and the birds came and ate it up. She envisioned the Scarecrow representing the "shallow ground," where the seed sprung up quickly but was burned up by the sun. Next, Jessie saw that the Cowardly Lion could represent the "thorny ground" that grew and choked out the seed due to the cares of this world. Lastly, she chose Dorothy to be the good soil, where the seed took root, grew, and produced a crop, a hundred, sixty, or thirty times what was sown. With the theme and the characters in place, the play *No Place Like Home* was born.

Several months after finishing the play, the Lord put it on Jessie's heart to turn it into a book, so that children all over could have a new way to have "ears to hear and eyes to see" what the Spirit of the Lord was saying through the parable of the sower. In a moment, the Lord showed her she was to partner with her friend, Janet Adele Bloss.

Janet was the perfect person to help Jessie turn the play into a book. Not only is Janet a published author of many children's books, but she also has fond memories of the original story, *The Wonderful Wizard of Oz* by L. Frank Baum. Janet's father (now ninety-nine years old) read the *Oz* books to her when she was a little girl. Writing about these characters and placing them into a new magical world was a labor of love.

We hope that you enjoyed this book and will pass it onto the precious children you know and love.

NO PLACE LIKE HOME READER'S GUIDE

Please use these discussion questions to prompt deeper discussion about the themes in *No Place Like Home*.

Before reading this book, how would you have described the Kingdom of God? Discuss.

Chapter 1

1) Have you ever been deeply disappointed by a close friend? Discuss what happened.
2) Do you ever talk to your dog, cat, or parakeet? Why do you think they make such good listeners?
3) Do you feel that you can be honest about your feelings when you pray?
4) As a Christian do you think it is all right to feel angry and disappointed at God sometimes?

Chapter 2

1) If you have a comforting scripture for when you're feeling anxious, please share it. If you don't have one, look at Philippians 4:5–6. How can we be anxious for nothing?
2) How does Ross try to help during a frightening situation?
3) How does Jay respond to the situation?
4) How does Chad respond?

Chapter 3

1) What do you think Dorothy is looking for in the Land of the Seekers?
2) Who is the Big Boss in the Sky and the Forever King? What is he like?
3) Has an unexpected situation ever happened so quickly that you weren't sure what to do?
4) What would be a good scripture to remember at a time like this?

Chapter 4

1) Why does Evileen want Dorothy to take the wide path?
2) Why does Princess Holly want Dorothy to take the narrow path?
3) What sorts of temptations can pull us over to the wide path?
4) Fill in the blanks from the last page of chapter 4:

"Don't _____," said Holly Sprite. "The crows are just trying to _____ you. Remember that Evileen and her crows are _____. You _____ _____ anything they say. They often mix truth with _____. That can be very confusing."

Chapter 5

1) What is the Tin Man most proud of?
2) What does *The Book of Wonderful Words* say about hearts?
3) If the Tin Man were to ask you, "How can you know someone with your heart?", how would you answer?
4) Why did the Tin Man quit walking along the narrow path with Holly Sprite?
5) What did the crows tell the Tin Man about the Kingdom of Heaven?

Chapter 6

1) Why does the Tin Man think that he could never be righteous?
2) What does Princess Holly give to D, the Tin Man, Pipken, and Harry? Can they ever lose it?
3) Can anything imperfect live in heaven?
4) 1 Corinthians 1:30 NIV – It is because of him that you are in Christ Jesus, who has become for us wisdom from God – that is, our righteousness, holiness and redemption. – What does this verse tell us about righteousness?

Chapter 7

1) The Tin Man doesn't need to eat like the others or rest or sleep. How does this make him feel?
2) Tin decides that if he wants to discover the Kingdom of God he can't just do nothing. What does he need to do?
3) What does Proverbs 3:5-6 say?
4) What does Isaiah 41:10-13 say?
5) What does Philippians 4:7 say?

Chapter 8

1) When Dorothy's mind begins to think over and over about sad things that have happened to her, how does that make her feel?
2) Who does Dorothy ask for help?
3) What does *The Book of Wonderful Words* advise Dorothy to replace her sad thoughts with?
4) What does Dorothy think about to get rid of her anxiety?
5) What does Philippians 4:8 say?

Chapter 9

1) How are Pipken and the Tin Man alike?
2) How do the crows try to influence Dorothy and her friends?
3) What does Evileen say about a loving God?

4) How does Evileen try to turn Dorothy's friends against her?
5) What new knowledge helps Dorothy to understand Pipken better?

Chapter 10

1) What do the crows keep telling the Scarecrow that makes him doubt himself?
2) Why did the Scarecrow leave the narrow path?
3) What did the crows promise the Scarecrow?
4) Why do the crows keep distracting the Scarecrow? What are they distracting him from?
5) In this chapter D says, "Princess Holly specializes in getting rid of _____ _____. That's why we _____ together. We _____ each other. We _____ each other. It's easier to not get scared and give up when you're with _____ traveling to the same place.

Chapter 11

1) "How can something so lovely be so dangerous?" Dorothy asks, when a flower tries to eat her head. How would you answer that question? What do you think might be lovely and dangerous?
2) Why would the Tin Man feel disappointed when he finds out that Scarecrow doesn't eat, doesn't sleep, and never gets tired?
3) Why do you think the Lion likes to have scary friends?
4) What are Chaos and Fear really good at?
5) What does Deuteronomy 31:6-8 say?
6) How can names that we call ourselves (or hear others call us) change the way we view ourselves?

Chapter 12

1) Why do you think the crows mostly pick on Scarecrow?
2) Why is it important to travel the narrow path with friends?

3) What does Proverbs 27:9 say about friendship?
4) What does Proverbs 18:24 say about friends?

Chapter 13

1) Where do Dorothy and her friends find themselves when they reach the end of the narrow path?
2) Why are they disappointed? What do you think they expected?
3) How do Evileen, Fear, and Chaos try to discourage the travelers?
4) Why do you think that Evileen, Fear, and Chaos are trying so hard to convince Dorothy that there is no Kingdom of God?

Chapter 14

1) When Fear whispers to the Lion, "Y-you'll never be b-brave," what does the Lion roar?
2) Why does Fear publicly talk about Pipken's "secret" deformity? How might this make Pipken feel?
3) Holly Sprite speaks with the same voice as _____ _____.
4) When people come to understand the depth of the Heavenly Father's love, they will be filled with four things. According to Tin, Scarecrow, the Valiant Lion, and Pipken, what are those four things?
5) How have the characters changed by the time they reach the end of the Narrow Path?
6) Fill in the blanks:

Dorothy clapped her hands. "Yay! Y'all are getting it. We learned that we are a _____ _____ once we decide to follow the _____ path and put our _____ in the _____ of Princess Holly Sprite."

Chapter 15

1) Does Dorothy think that her life will be without problems now that she understands who the Forever Father is, who Holly Sprite is, and what the Kingdom of God on earth is?
2) Which characters from the Land of the Seekers do Chad, Ross, and Jay remind you of?
3) When Tutu returns, what is in her beak? What does it symbolize?
4) When Dorothy explains to the boys her newfound understanding (of the purpose of life and of the Kingdom of God on earth), how do they react?
5) What different reactions might people have if you began to share your faith with them?
6) Fill in the blanks:

Dorothy, who knew better, calmly picked her path through the surrounding wreckage, her heart filled with peace and joy at the knowledge that a King and a Princess would always be with her. _____ and _____.

Now That You Have Read This Book
Discussion

1) How would you describe the Kingdom of God on earth?
2) Read the parable of the sower in Matthew 13:1–9 and 18–23. How does this parable apply to your life?
3) How has this book impacted you?
4) Who would you like to share it with?
5) What have you learned about the Holy Spirit from reading *No Place Like Home?*

ABOUT THE AUTHORS

Janet Adele Bloss is a nature lover with a huge imagination. An eleven-year-old at heart, she has written twenty-five books for children and young adults, including *Max and the Secret Skunk, The Haunted Hotel, Ballet Bunny, My Brother the Creep, The Haunted Underwear,* and *The Girl with Green Hair.* As a child, Janet was a voracious reader who slept with her books under her pillow at night, hoping the stories would stay with her. She enjoys jiujitsu, practices kickboxing, and likes chocolate a little too much. The three things she absolutely cannot live without are books, trees, and dogs.

With the publication of *No Place Like Home,* Janet hopes to reach a new generation of young readers and their parents with an allegorical adventure that reveals the Gospel message of hope and joy.

Jessie Beebe has been writing and performing plays since she was in kindergarten. She is a playwright, minister, performing arts director, and the president and founder of Stand Ministries. With a BA in elementary education and a specialization in theatre, Jessie flipped and ziplined through the air as Catwoman in a Batman stunt show and danced with Larry and Junior as the host of VeggieTales Rockin' Tour Live. As the leader of Stand Ministries, Jessie has traveled around the world, ministering and performing for kids of all ages. Jessie loves serving in ministry with her husband, Donny, and her two amazing girls, Ryleigh and Reese.

With the publication of *No Place Like Home,* she is excited to work with her friend, Janet, to transform the play she wrote into a book for the world to grow in their love for Jesus.

All proceeds from *No Place Like Home* go toward supporting Stand Ministries. For more about how to get children involved with performing arts that bring glory to God, go to www.StandMinistries.org.